PENNY JORDAN

without trust

Harlequin Books

TORONTO • NEW YORK • LONDON
AMSTERDAM • PARIS • SYDNEY • HAMBURG
STOCKHOLM • ATHENS • TOKYO • MILAN

Harlequin Presents first edition September 1989
ISBN 0-373-11201-7

Original hardcover edition published in 1988
by Mills & Boon Limited

CHAPTER ONE

'IT SHOULDN'T be long now.' Did he realise how un-
reassuring he sounded? Lark wondered as she listened
to the hesitant, slightly tense voice of her solicitor's clerk.
He probably wasn't much older than she was herself, a
young trainee whose work for a solicitor comprised, in
the main, Legal Aid cases, which had probably never
brought him into contact with a case of the notoriety
and severity of this one. No wonder he was looking at
her as though he half expected her to bare her teeth and
then sink them into him. That was what predators did,
wasn't it?

Predators! She shuddered and wondered if she would
ever fully be able to put behind her the events of the last
ten months. She would never be able to forget them,
that was for sure. The newspapers had had a field day
with the story, giving it intense coverage, and why not?
It was the sort of sordid tale that was almost guaranteed
to sell newspapers.

Would this affect her chances? Her solicitor had not
been able to reassure her that it would not, and perhaps,
after all, that was what she deserved for being trusting
and naïve. It amazed her that she still had the power to
feel such indignation after the tremendous battering her
self-confidence had received; and it had all started so
innocently. But who was going to believe that now? The
jury waiting outside to judge her? The 'other side' had
engaged one of the country's best-known prosecuting
counsels. She herself had never met him, of course, but
she had heard enough from her own solicitor to fear
him. If he could see to it that the jury condemned her,
he would. After all, that was his job.

That did not stop her feeling an almost irrational fear and hatred of him, though. Irrational because the person she really ought to hate was Gary, but somehow she couldn't do that. Perhaps it was the memory of the childhood years they had shared that stopped her from doing so, or perhaps it was the blood bond between them. She had no idea. She only knew that all her fear, all her hatred, all her anxiety, was focused on the inquisition she knew was to come; an inquisition that would be conducted by James Wolfe himself. She couldn't help shivering at the thought, her face pale and strained as she instinctively dipped her head forward in a defensive gesture so that it was shadowed by the curtain of her hair.

Only the previous week, her solicitor had begged her to give him the names of at least two character witnesses, who would strengthen their position, but how could she? Her aunt and uncle had refused to have anything to do with her. As far as they were concerned, she had ceased to exist, and in a way who could blame them? Her lips compressed and her companion, watching out of the corner of his eye, wondered if he dared tell her that her very obvious anger and resentment could only weigh against her.

Perhaps if she had looked different, pale and blonde maybe, instead of well tanned, her dark red hair curling riotously around her vivid face ... Lark would have told him that her tan came from helping out on the allotments alongside the railway lines. The work was therapeutic and helped to pass the time. Perhaps she ought to have tried to get a proper job instead, but how could she? She had no references, nothing. Only the odd sound penetrated through the thick doors shutting her off from whatever was going on inside the court room.

Even though she had been expecting it, had been tensely waiting for it in fact, when the door eventually opened and her name was called, it made her jump.

The walk to the witness box was a long one. Lark was burningly conscious of other people's curiosity. She refused to look anywhere other than at a spot somewhere above the judge's head. Because of the amount of money involved, this was a High Court action. The sight of so many gowned and bewigged officials was intensely intimidating.

Even so, she lifted her chin a little higher—a tall, slender girl whose face held the promise of mature beauty, but which at the moment was marred by tension and pride.

'Just look at her,' she heard someone whisper behind her, 'nose up in the air. You wouldn't think she'd be that brazen, would you? Not after what she's done.'

As she stepped into the witness box, Lark froze, her glance clashing with one of the bewigged lawyers. She had expected him to withdraw from the challenge under the hard stare of her dismissive eyes, something she had perfected over the long, hauntingly unhappy months, but instead she was the one to back down, to look away, a dark cloud of colour sweeping her skin as she did so.

He was tall, with dark hair showing under his wig, his skin almost as tanned as her own. His eyes were grey, a cool, unreadable grey that suggested that they knew a great many secrets. Who was he? Because she was so engrossed in him, she missed a few words the judge said, and therefore it was a shock to realise that he was coming towards her, although even then she didn't realise the truth until he addressed her in a cool, well-modulated voice, his words telling her exactly who he was.

James Wolfe, the prosecuting counsel, whom her solicitor had told her had been hired at an enormous fee by Crichton International to make sure she was seen to be punished for her crime. Counsel for the prosecution—counsel—she knew exactly what that meant now, just exactly how far up the legal ladder that title indicated this man was. Yet he couldn't be much over thirty—thirty-two or -three at the very most.

Her own counsel was much older, a dry, unsympathetic man, who had listened to her story as though he had found it boring and unbelievable. She remembered how frightened she had been then, realising for the first time just how alone she was, just how little anyone really cared. Certainly not enough to believe her, to understand.

The questions started, the story unfolding. Why were they bothering? Surely everyone in the country was familiar with them now? How her cousin had committed suicide on the eve of his employer's discovery that he had embezzled many tens of thousands of pounds from them by way of a complicated computer fraud. He had known he was about to be found out, that much was obvious.

The police had broken into his flat just after he'd taken the overdose. There had been long enough before he died for him to tell them the story that brought her here to this court today.

The story—the lies, didn't she mean? She had a shrewd idea why Gary had done it, of course, but who was going to believe her now? It had been three days before he'd died of liver failure connected with the effect of the tablets he had taken, a side-effect not known to many would-be suicides, and one which was just as lethal as the taking of the tablets themselves.

The police had remained at his bedside until he had lapsed into that final coma, or so she had been told. She had not been allowed to see him. Her aunt and uncle had been with him, of course. She had been waiting outside for them when they finally ended their long vigil.

She had never expected them to simply ignore her, never imagined they would believe Gary's lies. He was their son. Surely they knew how he liked to embroider, to deceive? But of course that wasn't the only reason he had told the police that he had stolen the money to give to her. He had said that it was her incessant demands, her threats of blackmail if he didn't comply with them, that had driven him to more and more embezzlement and finally to suicide.

What had started as a game had got out of control because she had forced him to steal more and more, or at least that was what he had told them. Only it hadn't been like that. She had had no idea what was going on; she had not even known about Lydia Meadows until she had seen the photographs in the local paper: a tall, elegant woman posing at the side of her much older husband, a very wealthy industrialist.

And then she remembered seeing Gary with her, a Gary who had obviously been completely besotted with her. Had she been the reason he had turned to crime? Had it been to protect Lydia that his dying words had been those lies which had brought Lark herself here today?

She admitted grimly to herself that she was probably never likely to know. After all, she wasn't going to get much chance to find out, locked away behind prison walls.

James Wolfe was still watching her, and she only just managed to repress the violent shiver of anguish trembling through her body at the thought of what today could lead to—prison. She wanted to cry and scream that they were wrong, that she had done nothing, nothing at all. Pride wouldn't let her.

Why would these strangers believe her when her own family would not?

She still couldn't believe how completely her aunt and uncle had turned against her. How they had never even for one moment allowed themselves to believe that their son might be lying—that she might be the innocent party. All those years when she had tried to think of them as her parents, when she had hoped they thought of her as a daughter, she had been living a lie. She knew that now.

It was hard not to feel bitter, not to feel resentful. But bitterness and resentment would get her nowhere now. No—what she needed was the skill of another James

Wolfe, skills that she somehow doubted she could find in her own tired and cynical counsel.

The cross-examination started and, although she was trembling inside, Lark held up her head proudly, her dark green eyes clashing with those of her attacker. How cool and controlled he was, how sure that he was going to win. She would be convicted. Such a large hammer to wield against such a very frail person as herself, but her cousin's employers were determined to make an example of her now that Gary himself was beyond their reach.

They and others like them were too vulnerable to embezzlement of this kind, and therefore they would want to ensure that no one else was tempted to follow in Gary's footsteps, that others saw exactly how harsh the punishment for such embezzlement could be. As an accomplice, her sentence would be comparatively light, of course—non-existent if she could convince the judge that Gary had lied. But, even as her solicitor had said those words, Lark had read in his eyes his own disbelief of her tale. After all, why should her cousin deliberately implicate her, a girl who had been brought up practically as his sister? What kind of man would do such a cruel and malicious thing to another member of his family? Certainly not a man as mild as Gary.

But there had been another side to Gary—one that the world did not see. One that was hidden and secret. It had been a long time since she had allowed herself to think of those first days when she had been orphaned, when Gary's parents, her aunt and uncle, had taken her into their home.

They had been unhappy, dark days, filled with longing for the parents she had lost. Days which had been further darkened by Gary's hostility towards her. Two years older than her, he had tormented her cruelly in those early months: getting her into trouble with his parents, stealing and destroying her toys, taunting her by telling her she would have to go and live in a home. But surely it wasn't just because of his childish resentment that Gary had lied about her now?

No—she was convinced that there was more to it than that. Convinced that Gary had lied to protect the woman he loved. A woman who was married to another man.

Caught up in her own emotions, she was intensely aware of the emotional climate of the court room, and of the way James Wolfe skilfully played on those emotions, when describing to the jury the enormity of her supposed crime.

It was the company shareholders, ordinary people much like themselves, who would ultimately be the losers, so he told them. People who put their life savings into companies such as the one Gary worked for. Life savings which had been stolen by a young man who was now beyond their reach. But he was not the real perpetrator of the crime. He had been forced into it, blackmailed by his cousin, by herself.

Sickly, Lark realised that the jury were drinking in every word, sitting in silence, deeply absorbed in everything that James Wolfe was saying to them. He was lying, lying to them, she wanted to call out. None of what he said was true. *She* wasn't the reason Gary had robbed his company. She wasn't the one he had wanted the money for.

What was the use of saying anything? Nobody would believe her.

Listlessly, she answered the questions he put to her, the words mechanical and without emotion. How many times had she already been through those questions? How many times had she already listened to the same words?

The cold grey eyes focused on her, and an unnerving sensation raced up and down her spine.

'What a very fortunate young woman you are, Miss Cummings. Tell me something, do you honestly feel no compunction, no guilt, no remorse?'

It was too much. Lark stared at him, her temper suddenly deserting her.

'No,' she told him recklessly, 'I don't feel any of those things. Not a single one. I don't need to. I'm not guilty. I haven't done anything. You don't understand. You're wrong, wrong!'

To her horror she discovered she was crying, her whole body shaking with the force of her emotions. There were sounds behind her, tuts from the jury, the vague sounds of unease the British always make in the face of other people's emotions.

Hatred engulfed her as she tried to control herself. He had done it deliberately—deliberately trapped her into saying what she really felt. She looked at him proudly, her head held up, her body trembling under the force of her feelings. Grey eyes looked back at her. She could read nothing in them, but then, what had she expected to read? Triumph, because he knew he would win his case? He was far too professional for that, she decided scornfully, watching him as he turned and walked away from her.

The rest of the proceedings passed in a blur. There were questions and then more questions. There were speeches and then more speeches, but none of it meant anything to her. She already knew what the outcome was going to be. No one had had such a profound effect on the jury as James Wolfe, no one had had as profound an effect on her.

Her solicitor was withdrawn and ill at ease when the case was eventually adjourned for a break. The jury had retired to make their decision. As she stood in the long, draughty corridor next to her solicitor, Lark shivered convulsively. Only now, when it was over, did she actually realise what was happening to her: this could be one of her last few precious hours of true freedom. Prison. She shivered, unable to contemplate the enormity of what was going to happen to her.

Why? Why, when she was innocent? But this was a case in which innocence had to be proved, and how could she prove hers when she had been condemned by a dying man?

A harassed-looking court official appeared and drew her solicitor to one side. She saw them looking at her and her heart sank. Had the jury made their decision already? Was that what they were talking about?

Her solicitor turned to her and excused himself. The judge wanted to speak to him, he told her. He was gone for what seemed to be a long, long time. His assistant tried to take her mind off things by talking to her, but Lark wasn't in the mood for chit-chat. In other circumstances, she might have been willing to make more of an effort. The young man was shy and meant well, but it was more than she could manage at the moment to respond to his inarticulate small-talk.

When her solicitor came back, he looked slightly flushed and rather surprised. He drew her to one side, his smile almost avuncular as he said jovially, 'You're a very lucky young lady, Miss Cummings. Crichtons have made a last-minute decision to withdraw their case. Apparently they've decided that the publicity your conviction would give them would not reflect well on them.'

'To withdraw the case...' Lark was practically stammering. 'But surely they can't just do that?'

'Not in normal circumstances,' her solicitor agreed. 'But...er...in this case the judge has decided...' He was plainly struggling to give her an explanation for this extraordinary turn of events, but Lark didn't care. All she cared about was the enormous feeling of relief sweeping away the fear and anxiety of the past long months. It was over. She wasn't going to prison. She was free, she could simply walk out of this court and never again have to hear another word about Crichton International or Gary. She could hardly believe it. Especially not after the way James Wolfe had so effectively destroyed her while she was in the witness box. After what he had done, she had felt quite sure that the jury would have convicted her to a life sentence in Russia's salt mines if he had asked them to.

How infuriated he must be by Crichtons' decision! He hadn't struck her as the kind of man who would enjoy having the rug pulled out from under his feet like that.

Added to a sense of relief was one of dizzy pleasure. He had been cheated of his prey. She had actually escaped the net he had woven so cleverly around her.

God, how she hated him! How she hated all men like him who preyed on those less fortunate than themselves, using their intelligence, their skills, their training, to earn themselves a very good living from the misfortunes of others.

He had not cared whether she was guilty or innocent. All he had cared about was his fee.

Her solicitor was saying something, but she hadn't really been listening. She turned to look at him, her eyes flashing with the force of her emotions. He took a step backwards and eyed her uncertainly. He had not wanted to handle the case right from the very beginning. It had been loaded with potential disaster, with problems and uncertainties. At the very best, all he had hoped to get was a conviction that took into account her youth and lack of a previous record. That Crichtons should suddenly and almost inexplicably decide to drop the case was something he had not anticipated at all, and even now he could hardly believe it had actually happened.

She was free. Really free, for the first time since Gary's death. Without a backward glance, Lark walked out of the court and into the spring sunshine.

The London streets were busy, heavy with the sounds of traffic, a muted dull roar which suddenly sounded as triumphant as the most triumphal of all hymns. She wanted to dance down the street, to embrace almost everybody she saw. She wanted to cry out to them that she was free, that the ordeal was over. And yet, would they understand? No.

Probably, like the jury, they would have condemned her too, had they been given the chance.

A week later she wasn't feeling anything like as euphoric. Reality had set in hard upon the heels of her initial exuberance. Since Gary's death she had been living in a small bedsit she had managed to rent, but she had very little money of her own.

According to her aunt and uncle, the money that her parents had left her had been virtually swallowed up by her education. After school she had gone on to university, where she had obtained a Business Studies degree, and then it had taken her six months to find her first job.

Her bedsit was cold and damp, and she grimaced bitterly to herself as she sat huddled over its one-bar electric fire. Who would have believed that twelve months ago she had considered herself to be one of the luckiest people she knew? She had just landed her first job with a prestigious PR firm in the city. The salary hadn't been very high, but the PR firm was a very high-profile one which handled a lot of famous names.

She had planned to stay there for two or three years to gain some initial experience, and then look for something better. When added to her salary and carefully eked out, the five thousand or so pounds that was left to her from her parents' money would have just about lasted until she had been in a position to look for something better, but now all that was gone.

She had lost her job almost as soon as the news had broken. Her boss had called her into his office and explained to her in cool and bitingly unkind words that a high-profile PR firm could not afford to carry an employee whose name was splashed so notoriously all over the front pages of the nation's gutter press. She had not been sacked, simply asked to resign.

That had been six months ago. Now there was virtually nothing left in her account at all. How on earth was she going to get another job, once any prospective employer learnt who she was?

She had an interview with her solicitor in the morning. He wouldn't tell her what it was about on the telephone. Simply that there were matters he had to discuss with her.

There had been an uproar in the press over Crichtons' decision to pull out of the case, of course. A spokesman for the company had made the astounding statement that, because of certain anomalies in the evidence, they had decided not to go ahead with the prosecution.

What anomalies? Lark wondered. As far as she could see, the case against her had been very definite indeed. Her solicitor had not been able to enlighten her, either. He had simply said that they had been very, very lucky indeed, and now, as far as the national papers were concerned, she was yesterday's news.

What had happened? What Gary had done to her would haunt her all her life, she knew that. She would never be able to escape from it, never be able to get a job, make an application for a loan, do anything without referring to the fact that she had once been considered to be guilty of causing another person's death. And, what was more, of forcing him to lie and steal from his employers.

She had even thought about changing her name. She was not by nature deceitful, and her pride scorned the subterfuge of deliberately lying to others. But what was she going to do—join the already long queue of young people living on state benefits? At this stage, she couldn't see that she had any other option.

Her room was poorly lit and even more poorly furnished. She shared a bathroom with the other inhabitants of the run-down Victorian terrace. The drains smelled and the bathroom walls ran with damp.

She could never go back to her aunt and uncle. They would never forgive her for Gary's death. They would never cease blaming her for what had happened to him, and she in turn would never ever be able to feel the same way about them again.

She had looked upon them as her parents. She had loved them and thought they loved her, even though she had always known that Gary, their own child, would come first. The last thing she had expected was that they would turn on her the way they had done. It had left her feeling as though her whole world had slipped out of focus, as though nothing had ever really been as she had imagined it.

Now what she really wanted to do if she was truthful with herself was to escape—but escape to where or to what? She had always been a rather solitary sort of person, perhaps initially because of her parents' death. The abrupt shock of suddenly finding herself alone in the world at the age of eleven had had a profound effect upon her. Both at school and then later at university, she had been wary of too close a contact with others, of making friends, of allowing other people inside her carefully erected barriers; perhaps because, subconsciously, she was frightened that they would one day desert her as her childish mind had considered that her parents had done.

Logically, of course, she knew that their deaths had not been their fault, but children's emotions did not respond to logic, and left scars which even adult analysis could not wholly remove.

Smart, businesslike clothes, bought for her new job and hanging on a free-standing rail in her shabby room, reproached her. Now it was hardly likely they would ever be worn. Certainly not for the purpose she had originally envisaged.

During the long, dark days when the court case was pending, she had taught herself to live just one hour at a time. To look no further than one hour ahead, if that.

In fact, there had been times when she had felt so depressed that she had wondered whether it was worth being alive at all, but she quickly dismissed such dangerous thoughts.

Life was a gift, she had reminded herself fiercely. A gift that must not be wasted the way Gary had wasted his. She shivered again, but this time not because of any lack of heat. What had driven Gary to do what he had done?

She had known, of course, that he had always been a weak character, someone who did not like taking the blame for his actions. She had discovered that when they were children. Whenever they had been naughty and about to be found out, he had always somehow managed to ensure that she was the one to shoulder the blame. She had not objected in those days—perhaps because she had known instinctively that his parents would always support him against her. Had she known that? The thought was vaguely shocking. Could it be that she had somehow taught herself to love her aunt and uncle because she felt that her love was what she owed them? Could it be that she had never really felt that depth of affection for them at all, just as they had never felt any true affection for her? Had they perhaps always resented having to take her in, a solitary child, orphaned by the death of her parents? Parents who had not had the foresight to provide financially for a secure future for her.

Her uncle had had a good job, but there had always been a consciousness of money in the household. She remembered that, when they were children, her aunt had constantly reminded them how much their clothes had cost, how much their food had cost. She had never thought about it before, but could this have been what had led to Gary's absorption with money? Could this have been what had led him into embezzlement?

Surely not! How many times over the past few months had she gone over and over the events leading up to

Gary's suicide? How many times had she queried what lay behind his actions? Had it simply been the fear of discovery? The knowledge that such discovery would lead to imprisonment? Or had there been something more— a more deep-rooted fear and unhappiness?

Despite the fact that his parents had spoilt him, they had not been physically affectionate adults. She remembered that, as children, she and Gary had constantly been reproved for demanding physical signs of affection.

Her parents had been different, and how she had missed their hugs and kisses during those first two years with her aunt and uncle! Gradually she had learnt to accustom herself to their differing ways. Gradually she had learnt to keep her emotions to herself, and realised that if she was to gain her aunt and uncle's approval she would have to learn a different code of behaviour.

How much of her true self had she repressed deliberately over those years? How much had she become the person that her aunt and uncle expected her to be rather than the person she genuinely wanted to be?

It was pointless thinking about that now. Nothing could change the past, but there was still the future, and somehow she was going to have to find a way to live through it. But how? No money; no job; no true home; no friends; no family. All she could see ahead of her was a black void of nothing.

It was true that she had made friends with some of the old men who worked the allotments down by the railway when, out of desperation, she had one day wandered down there from the Victorian terrace where she lived, looking for something to do.

She had stopped to chat to one of the men, and then later on had offered to help him with his weeding. The hard physical work had helped her over those initial, dark, early days when she had first discovered that Crichtons intended to prosecute her. One thing had led to another, and within a matter of weeks she had found that she was helping several of the elderly men work their plots. None of them knew who she was or what she was involved in, and there had been a certain kind of relief to be found in tugging up the weeds and digging the rich, moist soil.

Lark had discovered that she enjoyed gardening. Neither her aunt nor uncle really bothered much with the small, neat suburban garden that surrounded their house. Someone came in twice a week to mow the lawns and keep the beds tidy during the summer months, and once a month during the winter.

Her aunt and uncle preferred the small, select dinner parties they attended, the bridge games with their small coterie of friends. Their lives were very regimented, Lark now realised. It was something which she hadn't really been aware of before, but then, of course, she had been living away from home for some considerable time, first at university and then later in her bedsit.

Gary, too, had moved out of the parental home, but unlike her he had found a job in the local market town where his parents still lived. Crichtons had opened up there several years ago, with brand new offices, all based on computer technology, and Gary had soon found a niche for himself there, with his skill as an advanced computer operator. Quite where and when he had met Lydia Meadows, Lark didn't know.

When she had asked her aunt and uncle about Gary's relationship with the other woman, they had denied vigorously that he had ever known her, but that seemed improbable because Lydia was a local girl, albeit one who was several years older than both herself and Gary. Even so, Lark remembered reading several years ago in their local newspaper that Lydia won a nationwide beauty competition. She had gone from there to modelling, her name cropping up regularly in the local paper.

Her marriage to Ross Wycliffe, a local businessman, had been widely publicised. Ross was many years her senior, a widower with grown-up children of his own. He also had a reputation for being very shrewd and hardheaded in business. He was reputed to be a millionaire. Certainly the photographs that Lark had seen of Lydia showed a very soignée young woman dressed expensively in furs and jewellery. How on earth had Gary got involved with her, if involved he had been? He had been in love with her, that much had been obvious on the one occasion when Lark had seen them together.

She had gone home unannounced for the weekend, wanting to collect some books that were still in her bedroom at her aunt and uncle's. Her visit had just happened to coincide with a time when her aunt and uncle themselves were away on holiday, and so she had gone round to Gary's to ask him if she could borrow his key to his parents' house.

His car had been parked outside. When no one had responded to her knock, she had gone round to the back of the small, semi-detached house. Neither of the participants in the passionate embrace she had witnessed through the window of Gary's dining-room had been aware of her presence for several seconds. Indeed, she herself had been so stunned that it had taken her that length of time to realise that she was intruding, and she was just about to whisk herself away when Lydia Meadows had turned around and seen her.

Neither of them had been very pleased by her presence, and initially she had put that down to the fact that she had interrupted them. It wasn't until later that she realised exactly who Lydia was, and why she would not be too happy about someone seeing her making love with a man other than her husband.

She had tried to talk to Gary about it, knowing how his parents would feel about his involvement with a married woman, but their relationship was such that they had never been close, and he had brushed her off with a curt refusal to discuss the matter.

It had been obvious that he had loved Lydia, but had she loved him in return? And had it been for her sake that he had been stealing money from his company?

Sighing faintly, Lark reminded herself that it was pointless going over and over this old ground again and again, that nothing was to be gained from living in the past. It was over, and she would have to find a way of putting it behind her. She could never go back. Her aunt and uncle would never forgive her for what had happened. Both of them blamed her for Gary's death—perhaps in their shoes she would have felt the same, although she hoped she would have had more compassion, more insight into other people's feelings.

Over the years there had been many, many occasions when she had desperately longed for her own parents, but to long for them so desperately at twenty-two, when she was supposedly an adult, seemed rather ridiculous. But long for them she most certainly did.

Her thoughts switched abruptly from her cousin to James Wolfe. It was odd the way she couldn't get him out of her mind, couldn't quite prevent herself from thinking about him in unguarded moments, remembering the cool timbre of his voice, the reasoned logic of his arguments, the overwhelming, overpowering and illogical emotional turbulence he had aroused in her. Her passionate outburst in the court room still had the power to make her flinch inwardly, and to wonder at the way he had broken through her defences.

She had sworn to herself that she would never betray herself in that way, and yet, with a few well-chosen words, he had caused her to forget that promise and to cry out to the world how badly she felt it was treating her. Did he ever feel the guilt and compunction he had accused her of not feeling? Did he ever wonder what happened to the victims of his savage cross-examinations? Victims who, like her, could quite easily have been innocent. No, of course he wouldn't. Men like him never did, did they? Men like him... She shivered slightly.

There had been very few men in her life, and certainly none like James Wolfe. So why was it that the very thought of him caused this frisson of sensation to race across her skin, almost as though in some primitive way she feared him on a level that had nothing to do with their meeting in court? On a level that was purely emotional, and had to do with her being a woman and him being a man.

She told herself that she was being ridiculous, that she had allowed the atmosphere in the court to disturb her far too deeply, and that was why she was still so vulnerable at the mere thought of the man. But somehow the excuse didn't quite ring true.

James Wolfe had made an impression on her which no amount of stern self-lecturing could entirely dismiss. There had been something so male and vigorous about him, something that aroused and piqued her feminine curiosity. That was what one got for being a virgin at twenty-two, she mocked herself. Idiotic fantasies about strange men.

CHAPTER TWO

LARK was still thinking about James Wolfe when she walked from the tube station to her solicitor's office on the morning of her interview. A chance sighting of a dark-haired man sitting in an expensive car at the traffic lights caught her attention, and it wasn't until he turned his head to return her look that she realised that it wasn't James and that she was staring at him quite blatantly. She blushed and walked on, angry with herself; angry and disturbed.

It was time she put James Wolfe out of her mind. There was no point in dwelling on what had happened. No point in reliving the torment of those long minutes in court.

Oddly, it didn't help much telling herself that he was the one who had been vanquished. Over the recent months her solicitor's offices had become as familiar to her as her own shabby bedsit. They were up three flights of stairs in an ancient building that didn't possess a lift other than one that rather reminded Lark of a creaking, terrifying cage.

She had lost weight; the need to economise had meant that she had cut down on her food. It was quite frightening to realise how lacking in energy she was by the time she reached the third floor.

Her solicitor himself opened the door to her, which rather surprised her. Normally, she was made to wait a good fifteen minutes before being shown into the inner sanctum. But today the outer office was empty. The secretary had gone to lunch, he told her, noticing her curious glance.

'Lunch, at eleven o'clock in the morning?' Still, it was hardly any business of hers, although she did notice that

24

her solicitor seemed rather flustered and uncomfortable. She had had that effect on him ever since Crichton International had decided to pull out of the case, and she wasn't quite sure why.

'Sit down,' he told her, beaming at her and picking up a pile of manuscripts from the chair opposite his desk.

She did so unwillingly, wondering what on earth it was he wanted to discuss with her. By rights she ought to be out looking for another job. Only this morning she had happened to see her landlord, who had reminded her that the next quarter's rent was due.

With accommodation in London being so hard to come by, he was able to charge more or less what he wanted for her appalling room, and she knew that if she didn't produce the money within a very short space of time he would have no compunction at all in evicting her. She had the money but, once it was gone, what would happen to her then? She could manage this quarter, possibly the next quarter's rent, but after that...

Her solicitor was clearing his throat nervously and playing with the papers stacked untidily all over his desk. A cloud of dust rose from some of them, and Lark grimaced faintly. The office looked as though it could do with a good clean; there was grime on the windows and a film of dust on top of the filing cabinet.

'Er...I asked you to come in this morning, because I've been...er...approached by...' He stopped talking and fiddled again with the papers, ducking his head as though he wasn't quite sure what he was going to say.

'Yes?' Lark prompted him.

'Yes...an old client of mine, a widow whose husband has left her very, very comfortably circumstanced... She...um...she's the chairwoman of a small private charity, and she's looking for a young woman to help her with her paperwork. She wants somebody who would be prepared to live in. She's based in London, but spends some time in Boston. She is herself actually an American who was married to an Englishman.'

Lark frowned, not quite sure what the point of his long, rambling statement was, until he looked at her and said rather nervously, 'It occurred to me that such a position might suit you, Miss Cummings. I know you...er... had to leave your previous post.'

Lark stared at him, unable to believe her ears. Here she was worrying about how on earth she was ever going to find another job, and right out of the blue she was being offered one which, by the sound of it, also included accommodation. Or perhaps she had misunderstood him. She looked at him and said firmly, 'Are you sure about this? Would she want me under the circumstances, or doesn't she know?'

'Oh, yes, yes, she knows all about you,' he hastened to reassure her. 'Yes, she seemed most keen to interview you. She said you sounded just exactly what she had been looking for.'

It sounded too good to be true. Lark didn't move in the sort of circles where elderly ladies still employed live-in companions, but she was widely read and knew all about the pitfalls of such employment. Perhaps she would be expected to work twenty-four hours a day for nothing more than a pittance and her food. Before she could actually voice these fears, her solicitor went on hurriedly, 'The salary is excellent—really, very generous, and of course there will be no living expenses. All those will be included. Mrs Mayers always travels first class, and she assured me that when she travels you will travel with her.'

Lark raised her eyebrows and asked enquiringly, 'And does the charity pay for all this first-class travel?'

Her solicitor looked shocked. 'Oh, no, no, certainly not! As I've already told you, Mrs Mayers is independently wealthy. She's charming, quite charming, and you really are a very fortunate young woman in being offered such a post.'

Lark frowned, a little puzzled by his attitude. Initially she had gained the impression that he had been the one to recommend her for the job, and yet now it sounded as though he had doubts about her suitability. She was just about to question him further when his telephone rang. He picked it up, covered the mouthpiece and pushed a piece of paper over to her.

'That's the address,' he told her. 'I've arranged an interview for you for two-thirty this afternoon, although I don't think you'll have any problems. Mrs Mayers is quite convinced that you'll suit her.'

He turned away from her when he spoke into the telephone, making it plain that he expected her to leave. Feeling rather bemused, Lark did so. When she had come to see him this morning, the very last thing she had expected was the offer of a job—especially not one that sounded almost too like a fairy-tale, and too good to be true.

It probably *was* too good to be true, she admitted as she walked down three flights of stairs and out into the cool air. Although officially it was spring, it was still almost cold enough to be winter, the trees barely in bud. She shivered beneath the cold wind, wishing she could afford to go and sit somewhere warm and order herself a decent meal.

No cooking was allowed in the bedsits, but in reality all the tenants had their own small gas or electric rings. Hers was tiny and only really fit for heating up a can of soup or the odd tin of beans, neither of which was particularly tempting at the moment.

She was hungry, but lunch was a luxury she could no longer really afford. Would this Mrs Mayers really want to employ her? The salary her solicitor had mentioned had indeed been generous, far more generous than the amount she had been receiving with the PR company.

She had tried to ask him what her duties would be, but he had been very vague on the subject, saying that Mrs Mayers would explain everything to her. She felt oddly reluctant to go for the interview, which was ridiculous under the circumstances. Had the ordeal of the last few months scarred her so much that she was actually afraid of meeting new people? Afraid of seeing in their eyes the dislike and contempt she had already seen in so many people's eyes, including those of James Wolfe?

James Wolfe—there he was again, back in her thoughts. How on earth had he managed to get there, and how on earth was she going to get rid of him?

He had absolutely no right to keep on pushing his way into her life, into her mind, into her thoughts, she thought distractedly as she hurried down the street. It was barely twelve o'clock; two and a half hours before she needed to attend her appointment, but it was on the other side of London in St John's Wood...

Lark stood outside a pretty little Victorian villa that some rich man had probably built for his mistress. There was a time when St John's Wood had been notorious for such dwellings. Now, of course, it was eminently respectable and an area to which only the extremely wealthy could aspire.

Her particular destination was set behind a high wall. Lark tried the gates and then realised that they were locked. A discreet metal plaque set into one of the brick pillars startled her by bursting into speech.

'Do come in, Miss Cummings. We've unlocked the gates for you now.' The woman's voice was late middle-aged rather than elderly, pleasant, with more than just a hint of warmth. Had she heard it in any other circumstances, Lark would have felt immediately drawn to its owner. As it was she felt too nervous, too on edge to do anything than give a startled glance at the gates and then try them again.

This time, of course, they opened. The front garden was large by London standards. Early shrubs were just beginning to burst into blossom against the walls, crocuses were dotted here and there on the smooth green lawn. Despite its very obvious elegance, the house had an almost comfortable air about it.

A dark blue Rolls-Royce was parked discreetly to one side of the front door. Was she supposed to go to the front door, or should she go round the back? Lark wondered bemusedly. It was the kind of house that made one start thinking about such things. Her dilemma was solved for her when the front door opened.

She walked into the parquet-floored hall, and was immediately struck by the pleasant scent of sandalwood which greeted her.

'Ah, I'm glad you like it. Some people don't. I can't understand why, can you? It always makes me think of sailing ships and the China seas, possibly because originally sandalwood was from the Orient. Oh, dear me, please excuse my chatter, I'm always like this when I'm nervous, I'm afraid. Come on into the sitting-room.'

Was this her would-be employer? This small, pretty woman, with her pepper and salt curls and ingenuous smile? She barely reached her shoulder, Lark noticed as they both paused in the entrance to the sitting-room.

'Oh, I forgot to take your coat. It's so cold out, isn't it? I've lived in this country for nearly forty years, and yet I still miss our New England springs.'

The American accent was barely discernible, and had a twang with which Lark wasn't familiar.

'I wanted to invite you to have lunch with me,' Mrs Mayers was saying as she ushered her into a pretty sitting-room decorated in soft blues and yellows. A fire burned cheerfully in the grate, and Lark couldn't resist a soft exclamation of pleasure as she looked around her.

'I'm so glad you like it. My son doesn't approve at all. He thinks it's far too frivolous and feminine. Do come and sit down. I'll get Cora to bring us some tea, or would you prefer coffee?'

Her hostess was charming but rather obviously slightly dizzy, and Lark couldn't help wondering how on earth she had come to be the chairwoman of a charity committee. Surely such a role demanded great organisational skills?

It had been a long time since anyone had treated Lark
with such warmth and friendliness, and she found herself
responding to it like a thirsty plant soaking up rain. It
was several minutes before she could interrupt her hostess
for long enough to ask her exactly what the job would
entail.

For a moment or two Mrs Mayers looked rather vague.

'Oh, yes, the job. Well, my dear, here's Cora with the
tea.'

Cora proved to be a late-middle-aged woman with dark
hair and a round face in which brown eyes snapped
energetically and curiously. Mrs Mayers introduced them,
and Lark was very conscious of Cora's scrutiny as she
put down the tea tray.

'Cora's been with us for years,' Mrs Mayers told her
when the other woman had left. 'I don't know what on
earth I would do without her.'

'Mrs Mayers, the job...' Lark prodded gently.

'The job, oh, yes! Well, my dear, I can't tell you
exactly what your duties would be other than to say that
you would be acting as my personal assistant.' Suddenly
she sounded brisker, less vague. 'The charity's only a
small one. We have a branch here in London and another one in Boston, which is not, perhaps, as odd as it
seems.' A rather sad smile touched her face. 'My first
husband was, like myself, from Boston. Our families had
known one another for years.' She made a slight face.
'That's how it is in Boston. We're a conservative lot,
I'm afraid. I became involved with the charity after the
deaths of my husband and son. Both of them died from
an inherited genetic complaint. My husband knew
nothing about it. There had been cousins, other members
of the family who had died in their early thirties, but in
those days...' She shrugged, her eyes suddenly very sad.
'When John, our son, was born, neither of us had any
idea. He died when he was ten. In some cases the disease
is more progressive then in others. My husband died
twelve months later. He suffered such a lot, poor man,

not just from the illness itself, but from his guilt over what had happened to John. He said before he died that, had he known, he would never have married me.' She smiled again. 'Perhaps it is selfish of me to be glad that he did not.'

She said it with such quiet sincerity that Lark felt a lump rise in her throat. This woman was the antithesis of everything she had expected before she came for the interview. She realised now that she had been guilty of judging her on surface evidence alone.

'My husband was a wealthy man,' Mrs Mayers continued quietly. 'Very wealthy. I used some of the money he had left me to set up the charity. In those days my first thoughts were that perhaps somehow we might be able to find out what caused the hereditary defect which gave rise to his death and that of our child. Those early days were probably what saved my sanity, but that was a long time ago. Now it's very different. These days we're far better organised, and the money we've raised has helped with research into the causes and possible treatment for the deficiency. A lot of work has been done. We've now managed to isolate the genes that cause the problem, but there is still an awful lot more work to be done, which is where you and I come in, my dear,' she added briskly.

'My role of chairwoman involves me in having overall control of our fund-raising activities both here and in Boston. I think you already know that I spend part of the year over there working for the charity.' When Lark nodded, she went on quietly, 'I'm not a young woman any more, unfortunately. In fact, my son claims that I'm too old to be doing as much work as I do, but I'm loath to give it up, so he and I have compromised. He has made me promise to get myself an assistant, which is where you come in, my dear. I do hope you're going to take the job,' she added whimsically, 'because if you don't, I'm afraid my son is going to insist I give up a very important part of my life.'

Her son, she had said, which meant that she must have married a second time. Almost as though she had read Lark's mind, Mrs Mayers continued, 'I have been married twice. I was devastated when John died. He and our child were the most important things in my life. I thought I would never, ever recover from the blow of losing them, but then I met Charles.' She smiled reminiscently. 'He was exactly as I'd always imagined an English gentleman to be. He was a surgeon, and I was introduced to him by a mutual friend in Boston.'

'And you have just the one son?' Lark prodded, conscious of an air of sadness settling on her companion's face.

'Yes, it is probably just as well. He is a typical Taurean, incredibly stubborn, but I shan't bore you by being a doting mother and telling you how wonderful he is. Did your solicitor tell you that the job would involve living in?' she asked anxiously. 'I know that wouldn't appeal to most young girls these days, but I'm afraid that it's really a necessity. You see, sometimes, because of the very nature of the work I do, it means working odd hours. We hold a variety of charity events to raise funds, and I would want you to help me with all of those. Plus there's a great deal of correspondence which always needs answering. Does the thought of living in deter you?'

Deter her? If only Mrs Mayers knew! Lark thought wryly. She glanced round the sitting-room again, comparing its warmth and loveliness with the shabby bareness of her bedsit. What person in their right mind would prefer living in that to living in something like this—or rather, living alone, to living with someone like Mrs Mayers? Her stubborn Taurean son apparently did, because with the next breath she was explaining to Lark that there would only be the two of them in the house, plus Cora.

'It's very much an all-female household, I'm afraid. Do you have a...a boyfriend?'

She looked rather hesitant as she asked the question. Lark shook her head quickly.

'Would you like to see your rooms?'

Rooms? Lark felt as though she had wandered into some sort of daydream.

'Mrs Mayers,' she said gently, 'you do know who I am, don't you? You do know about the court case?' Suddenly she had had the uncomfortable suspicion that her solicitor had not been totally open and honest with this charming woman, and that she had absolutely no idea of Lark's recent history.

To her surprise, Mrs Mayers said quickly, 'Oh, yes, I know all about that. It must have been awful for you, my dear.'

'They weren't true—all those things they said,' Lark told her desperately. 'None of it was true. I'd absolutely no idea what Gary was doing.' To her chagrin, tears suddenly filled her eyes. What on earth was happening to her—giving way like this?

'My dear, you must try to put it all out of your mind. It's over. It was a terrible thing to endure, I know.'

'I could have gone to prison,' Lark sobbed helplessly, suddenly overwhelmed by the terror of those dreadful months. 'That's what he wanted to happen to me. He wanted me to be sentenced to prison,' she hiccuped between sobs.

'He?' Mrs Mayers questioned uncertainly, coming to sit beside her and putting a comforting arm round her shoulder.

'The prosecuting counsel,' Lark told her. 'He believed that I was guilty. I know he did. I could see it in his eyes.'

She looked up at Mrs Mayers, and was astounded to see a rather odd expression in her eyes—an almost guilty expression, she realised.

'No, no, I'm sure you're wrong. Oh, dear, let me call Cora and she can make us a fresh cup of tea. You mustn't get upset like this. You must put it all behind you and make a fresh start.'

But could she? Could she put it all behind her? Lark wondered miserably as she fished for a handkerchief and dried her face. What on earth had possessed her to break down like that, and in front of her prospective employer as well?

She refused the offer of a cup of tea and tried to restore what she could of her dignity.

'You will take the job, won't you?' Mrs Mayers implored. 'It would be such a relief to tell my son that I have found someone.'

She wanted to take it. The duties Mrs Mayers had outlined to her had seemed far more interesting than onerous, and yet she couldn't help feeling that she was taking advantage of the older woman's generosity. It was all very well for her to say that she knew all about the court case, but did she really realise the enormity of the crimes of which Lark had so nearly been convicted? And this son of hers, whom she seemed so in awe of, what would he feel about Lark working for his mother?

'I don't know. I think we should both think about it,' she managed to say, guiltily aware of the disappointment in her prospective employer's eyes.

'Oh, dear, I've gone and done everything the wrong way, haven't I? And I did so want you to take the job.'

'I want to take it,' Lark told her honestly. 'But I'm not sure if it would be fair to you. Does your son...?'

'The choice is mine,' Mrs Mayers told her, surprisingly firmly. 'And *you* are my choice, Lark.'

How reassuring those words sounded. How they warmed the coldness of her heart; a coldness which had grown steadily more intense over the months, starting with Gary's accusations and then her aunt and uncle's rejection of her.

What ought she to do? she wondered on her way back to her bedsit. She wanted desperately to take the job, but her conscience wouldn't let her.

Mrs Mayers' son didn't sound like the kind of man who would neglect to check up on his mother's prospective employee. And once he did and he discovered what had happened, surely he would not allow his mother to employ her. Could she take the risk of that kind of rejection? Would it be fair of her to expose Mrs Mayers to her son's anger when he discovered the truth?

And yet, being with her today was like being given a taste of warmth after enduring the most icy cold. Perhaps the work would not tax her skills and abilities to the full, but it would give her an opportunity to regain the self-confidence she had lost during the months leading up to the trial. It would give her the chance to put the past behind her and start life afresh.

People in the kind of circle Mrs Mayers obviously moved in were hardly likely to concern themselves with the affairs of a young woman such as herself. There would be no knowing looks, no questions.

She let herself into her bedsit and was immediately struck by the contrast to Mrs Mayers' sitting-room. Her aunt and uncle's home was comfortably furnished, but it lacked the warmth that Mrs Mayers' home possessed.

Stubborn was how she had described her son, and yet, listening to her, Lark had known immediately how much she loved him. It was there in her voice, in her smile. She had once known that kind of love, before her parents' accident.

If there was one thing she detested, it was people who consistently felt sorry for themselves, she told herself fiercely. And yet it was through no fault of her own that she had become involved in Gary's dishonesty.

Gary had escaped from the consequences of what he had done, but he had unfairly left *her* to face them. Deliberately, or simply because he had panicked and known no other way of protecting his mistress? Lark was convinced that Lydia Meadows *was* his mistress, just as she was convinced that it was for her benefit that he had been stealing from his company.

But Gary was dead, and she would have to stop thinking about the past and put her mind on the future.

She sat down tiredly. Could she take the job with Mrs Mayers? And what about Mrs Mayers' son?

She had been aware of a slight inflection of uncertainty in Mrs Mayers' voice when she spoke about him. Did that mean that she herself was not sure that he would approve of her choice of employee? If he did not, where would that leave Lark?

Mrs Mayers had assured her that the decision was hers and hers alone, but it had been obvious to Lark that she respected her son, and no doubt valued his judgement...

Her head was starting to ache, and she pressed the palm of her hand to her temple wearily. She couldn't make a decision now. She would have to sleep on it. She wished there was someone with whom she could discuss what was happening—a friend whom she might confide in. But she had no close friends.

Her aunt and uncle had frowned on her bringing friends home when she lived with them, and those friends she had made at university had now all gone their separate ways.

She hadn't been in her new job long enough to make new friends. Or was it simply that her aunt and uncle's reluctance to admit new people into their lives had rubbed off on her, and that she had been wary of allowing anyone to come too close to her? She had once been accused of that by one of the young men she had met at university. But friendship hadn't been what he'd wanted from her.

At six o'clock she made herself beans on toast—a meagre meal that would have to suffice until breakfast the following morning. Her slenderness was getting very close to the point where she was almost becoming thin. If she took the job with Mrs Mayers she would never have to worry about where her next meal was coming from...She refused to listen to the tempting inner voice.

She wasn't going to take the job simply for selfish reasons. She had liked Mrs Mayers too much to do that. She could help the older woman, she knew that. From a quick glance at the files Mrs Mayers had shown her, she had realised that they were in a muddled and disorganised state, but she had felt that there was something that Mrs Mayers was holding back, something that was worrying the older woman, and she very much suspected that that something was Mrs Mayers' son's reaction to the news that his mother was employing a young woman who had only by the skin of her teeth escaped receiving a prison sentence.

She remembered how evasive Mrs Mayers had been when she had asked her about her reasons for approaching her with the offer of this job. Lark suspected that the truth was that Mrs Mayers had somehow or other learned in conversation with her solicitor what had happened, and that out of the kindness of her heart she had immediately and unthinkingly suggested that she could offer Lark a job. That was the kind of woman she was.

But Lark felt that she owed it to her to point out the problems that she might be storing up for herself by taking her on. And yet wasn't the job exactly what she needed? And with the added benefit of living accommodation thrown in as well?

It wasn't just the luxury of the house that drew Lark. It was the warmth that seemed to pervade it. A warmth that she guessed sprang from Mrs Mayers herself. Lark had found herself wishing that she might have had an aunt or a godmother like the American woman. Someone to whom she could have turned when her parents were killed.

How cold and withdrawn her aunt seemed when compared with Mrs Mayers. Or was it simply that she herself was far more sensitive to such things since the ordeal of the last few months? It was true that since she had grown up there had been an enormous distance between herself and her aunt and uncle, but she had put it down to the fact that she was growing up rather than to any lack of emotion for her on their part.

Now she knew the truth. They had never loved her in the way that she had always believed they did. In fact, they had resented her, and very deeply. That had been made abundantly clear to Lark following Gary's death.

It didn't take her long to clear up after she had eaten. She was still wearing the clothes in which she had gone for her interview. She ought to change out of them and press them so that they would be ready to wear the next time that she needed them. If she ever needed them again...

She had just changed into an old pair of jeans and a warm sweatshirt when she heard someone knocking on her door. Visitors were such an unusual occurrence that it was several seconds before she could actually accept the fact that it was her door which was being knocked on.

She went to open it and then hesitated uncertainly. While she hesitated, the knocking increased in volume, its imperative summons demanding that she open it immediately.

The man standing there was instantly familiar to her, but the shock of seeing him so totally unexpectedly robbed her of the ability to do anything other than simply stand and stare, her heart giving a gigantic leap and the breath squeezing out of her lungs as she looked into James Wolfe's cool grey eyes.

Her first panicky thought was that somehow or other there had been a mistake and that he had come to drag her back to court. Her fear of that thought was so great that she actually started to try to close the door.

But, as though he had anticipated such an action, he stepped into the room, forcing her to move back or risk coming into physical contact with him. If he had appeared formidable in court, it was nothing to the effect he was having on her senses now.

Somehow, being stripped of his court robes had invested him with an even more intensely masculine aura. As he reached out to push her door closed behind him, her attention was caught by the sinuous strength of his wrist. A gold watch glinted discreetly in the dim light of her room.

She watched him tensely, unable to understand what he was doing here, and yet too shocked to frame any coherent questions.

'You should never open your door without finding out who's on the other side of it,' he reproved her casually. 'Not these days—not in London.'

Weakly, Lark collapsed on to her shabby, lumpy settee.

'What are you doing here?' Her voice sounded cracked and strained, artificially high and totally unfamiliar. She noticed that her hands were shaking and, to hide it from him, she folded them and tucked them underneath her. She didn't want to betray any weakness in front of this man, but she realised immediately that he had seen the small, betraying gesture.

Something flickered in the depths of his eyes. Triumph? No, it hadn't been that. Then what? Compassion? No, never, not from a man like James Wolfe.

'What are you doing here?' she repeated huskily. 'Or can I guess?' she demanded bitterly, her brain suddenly working properly. 'You hated it, didn't you, that the case was dismissed? You wanted them to convict me.' Suddenly she was back inside the court room, the silence around her charged with expectations, as the jury waited for her to respond to his allegations.

She drew a quivering breath, unaware of his frown as he studied her, unaware of anything other than the terror of the moment when she had known that no one would believe her. That, innocent as she was, innocence on its own was not going to be enough.

'Well, there's nothing you can do about it now,' she told him harshly, dragging herself back to reality.

There was a moment's silence, and then he asked quietly, 'Is that how you're going to spend the rest of your life? Living in the past?' His question startled her. It wasn't the reaction she had been expecting at all, but before she could say a word he continued derisively, 'But then, what else can you do, living here? You don't have a job, you don't have anything, do you?'

He had come here deliberately to taunt her, to remind her that, although she might have escaped conviction, she was still being punished as he quite obviously considered that she should be. But he was wrong, she did have a job.

Lark didn't stop to weigh the consequences, to remember how she herself had had doubts about the wisdom of accepting Mrs Mayers' generous offer. Instead she told him with fierce pride that he was wrong, that she did have a job. Her eyes flashed fierce signs of fire, her hands clenching into small fists as she stood up to face him.

He didn't look as surprised as she had expected, but then, of course, he was adept at concealing his true feelings; that would have been all part of his barrister's training.

'You see, despite what you tried to do to me, there are still people around who can recognise the truth when they hear it.'

An odd expression crossed his face. If she hadn't known better she might almost have believed that he was amused, and then suddenly he leaned forward, his hand touching her throat, sliding up over her skin to her jaw, cupping it firmly.

The shock of his unanticipated touch scalded her into immobility, while her pulse jumped frantically beneath her skin and her heart surged heavily against her breastbone. She knew that he was going to kiss her, and yet she refused to believe it. It was unthinkable, impossible, unimaginable, and yet when his mouth touched hers it was as though some part of her had always known that one day there would be a man who would kiss her like this, who would make her pulses race and her blood burn, who would caress her mouth with his own, and in doing so possess her more thoroughly than any other man before or after him.

Her senses reeled beneath the force of it, her mind a total blank, as he kissed her with slow thoroughness, not rushing or forcing her, his mouth tasting hers with voluptuous delight. His hand still supported her neck, his thumb gently caressing her pulse. His body didn't touch hers. He made no move to hold her closer or to touch her in any other way, and yet she trembled as much as though he had caressed every single inch of her.

He released her slowly and deliberately. She came back to earth to hear him saying softly, 'Delicious.'

Her eyelids felt weighed down. It was an effort to open them and look at him. He was smiling at her, his mouth curving half mockingly. His eyes looked more silver than grey, liquid like mercury.

She wanted to reach out and trace the shape of his mouth in wonder and awe, still lost in the mystery of what had happened between them, and then he said in amusement, 'What's wrong, Sleeping Beauty? Has no one ever kissed you before?' And immediately she realised exactly what she was doing and wondered how on earth she would ever be able to forgive herself for being so stupid.

'You had no right to do that,' she told him painfully, appalled by the folly of her own actions, and yet her heart was still thumping, the effect of his touch still bemusing her senses. She *had* been kissed before, of course, but never in a way that had affected her so strongly.

'No right at all,' he agreed affably, cutting across her thoughts. 'But that didn't stop both of us enjoying it.'

Enjoying it? Lark almost choked on her chagrin, but what could she say? She *had* enjoyed it, more than enjoyed it, she admitted, shivering as she remembered how she had abandoned herself to the sensation of his mouth moving against her own.

It was because it had been such a shock, she told herself defensively. For him to kiss her had been so out of character, the very last thing she had anticipated.

'I want you to leave,' she told him stiffly, standing up and walking over towards the door. Her whole body felt as though she had been subjected to a terrible fever, her joints actually feeling as though they ached. It wasn't a pleasant sensation.

To her relief he made no demur, but it wasn't until he had actually gone and she had locked the door behind him that she realised that she had never really discovered exactly why he had come in the first place. What if he should come back? Panic hit her. She didn't want to see him again. She couldn't. She couldn't even think about why she was so terrified at the prospect.

There was only one way she could escape. She would have to take Mrs Mayers' job. Even if he traced her there, she wouldn't be so alone, so vulnerable. He would never kiss her like that while she was living with Mrs Mayers. He would never dare to arrive on Mrs Mayers' doorstep and demand entrance.

Had his kiss been his personal way of extracting payment because the case had been cancelled? She shivered, hugging her arms tightly around herself.

He was certainly arrogant enough to do something so unorthodox, but there hadn't been anger in his touch, nor resentment. So why, then? She shivered again, knowing the answer but not wanting to admit it. There had been that brief moment of time in the court room, that exchanging and mingling of glances that had contained more than mere acknowledgement of one another as adversaries.

Too inexperienced to judge its value properly, she had nevertheless been aware of that brief arcing of some indefinable emotion between them, some sensation of almost physical communion, generated by their mutual awareness. But she had dismissed it, not wanting to recognise its potential.

She shivered, wrapping her arms around herself for instinctive comfort. She would have to take the job now. She wasn't going to allow herself to dwell on exactly why she felt this need to protect herself, and if Mrs Mayers' son disapproved, well, that was his problem, she told herself defiantly.

CHAPTER THREE

WHY on earth was she spending so much time agonising about taking the job which, in her heart of hearts, she was forced to admit might have been tailor-made to get her out of her present dilemma?

The reason was quite simple. She liked Mrs Mayers. The older woman had stressed right from the start that she knew all about the court case and that she didn't want to discuss it.

Lark had taken her words at face value, only too glad to meet someone at last who was prepared to judge her on herself and not on what she had read in the papers about her. But would the same hold true for Mrs Mayers' son? Somehow, she doubted it very much, and there was the crux of her dilemma.

With every word she had said to Lark about her son, Mrs Mayers had betrayed her love of him, and mixed with that love had been just the tiniest tinge of awe, Lark was sure of it.

She wouldn't go as far as saying that Mrs Mayers was in fear of her son. Lark would hate to be the cause of any trouble between them, and yet, if she didn't accept Mrs Mayers' offer, what on earth was she going to do? And that was before she had even begun to try and analyse exactly why James Wolfe had come round to see her.

She told herself that she had hated the way he had brazenly demanded entrance to her flat, the way he had so calmly and arrogantly assumed that she would welcome his attentions. Attentions! She laughed bitterly and wryly to herself.

What a very old-fashioned word for what was in effect a very modern sin. She had no doubt at all about what

James Wolfe had wanted from her. She remembered with sick distaste several newspaper men who had haunted her doorstep until they realised that there was simply no way she was going to respond to their advances.

They had been at first amused and then annoyed to discover that she was not in the least flattered by their propositions. She had been astounded to discover that they seemed to take it for granted that she would be only too happy to go to bed with them. Common sense had warned her that they would laugh in her face if she had told them she was simply not that kind of girl, which happened to be the truth.

She was twelve years old when her aunt took her on one side and gave her a lecture about the ways that good girls did and did not behave. Her aunt had left her in no doubts whatsoever as to what her fate would be if she ever dared to stray from the straight and narrow path she had just outlined to her.

As a teenager, Lark had struggled with her own inner rebellion when she'd discovered her cousin was not expected to adhere to the same rigid moral code. Now she considered it was too late for her to indulge in the kind of teenage experimentation she had then been denied.

At university, she had been too busy to have much time to spend with friends of the opposite sex. In her first month at work, she found that she had discovered a certain fastidiousness that put her out of step with many of her peers. Perhaps that was why the thought of working for Mrs Mayers was so tempting. It would be a totally non-threatening environment—something that she needed badly after the traumas of the past few months. Something that she needed badly because it would provide an escape from James Wolfe.

She shivered a little, cross with herself for allowing him to creep into her thoughts. She could still feel the imprint of his mouth on her own, still see his lazy amusement at her shock. What had been his purpose in coming to see her? One thing she was sure of, she wasn't going to wait around for him to appear a second time so that she could ask him.

For all she knew, he could be like the newspaper men she had met, making a habit of taking his victims to bed. Well, in her case he was going to be disappointed.

She tried to imagine him making the virulent comments she had been subjected to by the reporters, but somehow couldn't quite do so. He was too controlled, too much in charge of his emotions to do that.

She tried to visualise him losing his temper and was dismayed with herself for doing so.

Morning brought her no closer to a solution to her dilemma, until her landlord arrived and announced that he was intending to put up her rent. Lark hated the way his eyes roved unceasingly over her body while he talked to her. She had never liked him, right from the start, and last night's episode with James Wolfe had left her feeling acutely vulnerable.

Her flat was nowhere near as safe as she would have liked. The rent the landlord mentioned was exorbitantly out of line with the accommodation. She told him as much, and flinched as he sneered, 'A woman like you—you'll soon find the money from somewhere or someone.'

Dear God, was this what she was going to have to put up with until the world forgot about who she was and what had happened? It wasn't until she heard herself telling the landlord exactly what he could do with his rent increase and his accommodation that she realised that she had committed herself to Mrs Mayers' job.

Shaking with reaction, as soon as the landlord had gone she pulled on her coat and hurried out into the street to the nearest telephone box.

Mrs Mayers answered the telephone herself. Shakily, Lark told her her decision, unable to keep the hint of apology from her voice as she did so. She only hoped that the older woman would not live to regret her generosity. She would have felt better if she had actually met Mrs Mayers' son before accepting the job, but he was a very busy man, Mrs Mayers had informed her, and a touch of defiance in her voice as she said the words had made Lark condemn him as both overbearing and selfish.

No sooner had Lark told Mrs Mayers that she was accepting the job than the latter was asking if she could start work almost straight away.

'I've been trying to organise a charity "do" to make money for more research,' she told Lark apologetically. 'I've thought of farming everything out to one of those agencies who specialise in organising such events, but it's going to cost too much money, and so I need your help desperately, Lark, to get everything sorted out. J— my son inherited a beautiful house near Oxford from his uncle. It's far too big really for a bachelor, but it has the most marvellous grounds and ballroom, and he's very kindly agreed that we can make use of both.'

The tone went, and Lark had to put more money into the telephone. Hurriedly Mrs Mayers said, 'Look, it's silly of me trying to tell you all this over the telephone. How quickly could you move in here, Lark?'

How quickly? Right away, if the truth were known.

Before she could say a word, Mrs Mayers continued, 'I know it's pushing you dreadfully, but how about tomorrow morning? I could send Harold round with the car to help you transport all your things, if that's any help.'

Lark tried to demur, to insist that she would manage somehow, but Mrs Mayers overruled her.

'Good heavens, child, it's no trouble, no trouble at all. Harold complains that he hardly ever gets to drive me anywhere as it is. He will be grateful to you for giving him the opportunity to give the car an airing.'

Lark didn't argue. She wondered if there was something wrong with her that she should so easily allow herself to be wrapped in the cotton-wool caring of Mrs

Mayers' kindness. Perhaps it was because she had lost her own parents so young, or perhaps she was just a weak-kneed idiot who hadn't the guts to stand on her own two feet, she challenged herself, as she agreed to Mrs Mayers' suggestion and replaced the receiver.

In the past she had not been called upon to question her strength of character or potential lack of it. These past few months had taught her things about herself she might otherwise never have known, had freed her from the obligation that had been hers from early childhood to love the aunt and uncle who stood in the place of her own parents. Mingled with the guilt and unhappiness she had experienced on learning that they had never really liked her, never really wanted to give her a home but considered it to be their duty, had been relief in the knowledge that now at last she was free to be her own person.

What did she really want from life? That was easily answered. Security. The kind of emotional security she had lost with her parents. A relationship with someone who loved and trusted her, and who did not require her to act a part that was foreign to her nature. In fact, she derided herself, she wanted what almost every other young woman of her age wanted.

As she walked up the stairs to get to her bedsit, the landlord was on his way down. She had to practically squeeze against the wall to avoid coming into physical contact with him. There was a smirk on his face that made her feel almost afraid. Thank God she was leaving in the morning!

She had never really liked the man, but it was only recently that she had become aware of the way he had watched her and been frightened by it. No doubt James Wolfe would be amused by it.

James Wolfe—there he was again—walking into her mind as though he had every right to be there, dominating her thought processes with the same subtle skill with which he had dominated her physically last night.

Knowing that Mrs Mayers' chauffeur was due to arrive at eleven in the morning, and determined not to trespass on her generosity more than was absolutely necessary, Lark decided to save him the journey by arranging for a cab. She spent the rest of the evening sorting through her belongings. There weren't very many. The precious photograph albums that dated back to her parents' engagement and marriage, and then followed the early years of their marriage: featuring places and people whom in the main she did not know, but whose faces were precious to her because they had shared her parents' lives, if only briefly.

With a maturity she had not possessed as a child, she recognised how significant it was that none of those photographs featured her aunt and uncle, apart from the formally posed 'group' pictures of her parents' wedding. The relationship between sister and brother had obviously not been a close one but, when her parents died, they had been her only family, and had been obliged to take her in out of duty.

She sighed faintly and put aside the albums, including the especially precious ones that followed her own birth. If she ever needed to be reassured that she had been loved, she only had to turn these pages, and see the radiant joy and pride in the faces of her young parents.

One small box contained all that was left of her childhood toys and books. She had been horrified on returning from university to discover that her aunt had burnt the rest, considering it ridiculous that a young adult woman should want to hang on to such rubbish.

Three dog-eared 'Peter Rabbit' books, a doll with one arm missing and a battered teddy bear, plus an assortment of dolls house furniture in various stages of dilapidation, were all that was left.

She touched them lovingly, her eyes misting. Would she ever again recapture the security and joy she had known as a child? Did any adult?

When she had children, she would do all that she could
to give them that same love and security. Her own father
had been a man out of his time, who had enjoyed playing
with his small daughter, and who had not left her care
completely in the hands of her mother.

With another sigh she put aside the box. Sitting here
reminiscing was wasting precious time. She wanted to
be up and ready to leave first thing in the morning. Her
sturdy independence, which had suffered such stunning
blows during the months leading up to the trial, was once
again beginning to surface. Mrs Mayers' faith in her had
restored something to her she thought she had lost for
ever.

The rest of her packing took very little time. She had
no furniture of her own; just her clothes, and the silver
dressing-table set which had come down to her from her
mother, who had in turn inherited it from her own
grandmother.

It was delicate and Edwardian. It was also very
valuable, and her aunt had been none too pleased to
learn that Lark intended taking it with her when she left
for university.

Following her realisation of exactly how her aunt felt
about her, one or two niggling questions had raised
themselves in Lark's mind.

What had happened to the several valuable antique
pieces of furniture she remembered her mother pol-
ishing so lovingly while she explained that they had come
down to them from both her own and Lark's father's
family? Lark's aunt and uncle had always maintained
that there had been barely enough money from the sale
of the house to pay for Lark's clothing over the years,
never mind anything else, but her parents had owned a
very pretty Chelsea home, and she remembered her
mother as always being well dressed and her father
driving a good car.

But what was the use of worrying about a problem
she could never totally resolve? And, whatever small un-

kindnesses had been inflicted on her by her aunt and uncle, they could be nothing when compared to the anguish they must be suffering now, especially her aunt, who had doted on her only child.

It was just gone eleven when she went to bed; the sound of footsteps on the stairs outside her room made her tense nervously. They paused, and her mind flashed back to the previous evening when James Wolfe had visited her so unexpectedly.

But whoever had lingered outside her door moved on, and eventually she was able to sleep.

She had set her alarm for six; just in time to hear the sleepy dawn chorus of London's starlings.

Everything was packed; her possessions looking very meagre indeed. All she had to do now was to shower and dress, then have her breakfast; by that time the mini cab she had ordered the previous evening should have arrived.

One thing she would definitely not miss about her accommodation was the grimy bathroom she shared with the other occupants of her floor. No matter how much money was expended on cleaning products, the bath remained a dirty, dingy grey; the walls were damp, and one of the other girls swore that if one walked into the room without switching on the light it was infested with cockroaches. Lark shuddered at the very thought as she showered quickly under the meagre water supply. She and the other girls had clubbed together to buy two large bolts for the bathroom door, but even so, Lark didn't like lingering in the unappealing surroundings.

By half-past seven she was ready, the small fridge cleaned out and the room bare of all her possessions.

Just as she was beginning to get jittery and have second thoughts about the wisdom of what she was doing, the cab arrived.

One of the first things she must do, she reminded herself as she helped the driver load her boxes, was to get in touch with her solicitor and thank him for his good offices on her behalf. She could still hardly believe that he had been so thoughtful. It seemed oddly out of character with the rest of his behaviour. She must have misjudged him, she decided, sinking thankfully into the cab when the last of her things were loaded.

She had planned to arrive at Mrs Mayers' at around eight o'clock, not too early to disrupt the household and yet in plenty of time to prevent the chauffeur from making a needless journey.

As it was, she was glad she had allowed herself some time in hand, because roadworks were causing traffic delays, and it was closer to eight-thirty than eight when the cab eventually set her down outside the house.

Front door or back? Lark mused as she asked the driver to wait. Her dilemma was solved when the gates and the front door opened simultaneously and Mrs Mayers' housekeeper came out. Her eyebrows rose a little when she saw Lark, but when Lark explained that she had wanted to save the chauffeur an unnecessary journey, a look of approval softened the other woman's features.

'That was very thoughtful of you,' she told Lark. 'Not that he would have minded collecting you for one minute. I'll give him a shout and he can give the cab driver a hand with your things.'

'There's no need for that,' Lark told her firmly, softening her words with a warm smile. 'I'm sure I can manage, if you could just point me in the right direction. Mrs Mayers did show me my room, but I'm afraid I can't remember where it was.'

Again she was given an approving look. 'Well, if you're sure you can manage...'

'There isn't anything heavy, and the cab driver will give me a hand.'

She glanced through the front door at the immaculately polished parquet floor and the pastel stair carpet.

'Is there another staircase? Some of the boxes are rather dusty.'

'Yes, there is. If you like I'll show you the rear entrance; your driver can get right up to the door there.'

It didn't take long for Lark and her driver to unload her things. She tipped him generously, more generously than she could really afford, she admitted ruefully, remembering how little there was in her bank account.

Her room was lovely, large and square, on the corner of the building with one window overlooking the charming back garden, and the other the flagged parking area and garages to the side of the house.

In addition to the bed, dressing-table, and huge fitted wardrobes, there was also a pretty Victorian writing-desk with a matching chair, and a reproduction cupboard which she discovered contained a television and video.

There was an attractive round table, ornamented by a bowl of spring flowers, and at the bottom of the bed a two-seater settee so that the room served as a sitting-room as well as a bedroom.

Its décor and furnishings were all like something out of a glossy magazine: pretty, soft, country-house chintzes with expensive designer details such as toning linings and appliquéd cushions. This was not the kind of room normally made available to employees, surely? It was more like a luxurious guest-room.

A door off it had been left open to reveal her own private bathroom. Nothing like the bathroom at her bedsit. This one had pretty curtains to match those in her bedroom. Immaculately white sanitaryware, and fitments toning in with the bedroom's colour scheme.

The same delicate peachy-pink pastel carpet that covered the floor in her bedroom flowed through into the bathroom. In the bedroom it had a bordered edge in dark blue to tone in with the fabric of the curtains and bedspread. The radiator was hidden behind a painted screen, and the window that overlooked the garden had a charming windowseat covered in the same material.

She heard a clock striking the hour and wondered what she should do. Go down and present herself to Mrs Mayers, or unpack and wait to be summoned?

She was just debating the matter when her bedroom door opened, and Cora came in with a tray of coffee and biscuits.

'Mrs Mayers will be ready to show you the study in half an hour. I brought you this...' She put down the tray.

'You're spoiling me,' Lark told her. The coffee was obviously freshly brewed and smelled heavenly. 'I'm afraid I'm a little out of my depth here,' she admitted frankly. 'In my previous job, I was working in an office, not a private house. Can you give me an idea of Mrs Mayers' routine? Obviously I don't want to intrude on her private time...'

'She doesn't have a routine as such. Works far too hard, she does...' Cora scowled. 'And I'm not the only person to think so. It's high time she had someone reliable to help her. Not at all well she was last winter. She has a weak heart, but she won't listen to sensible advice. I've told her, there's no sense in killing herself. What good will that do anyone?'

Lark frowned. She hadn't realised that Mrs Mayers suffered from ill health, and said as much to Cora.

'No, you won't do,' the housekeeper told her. 'She's not the sort to make a fuss, isn't Mrs Mayers. If you ask me, that's why you're here... To make sure she doesn't try to do too much. That will be Mr...'

She broke off as they both heard the telephone ring, and the housekeeper excused herself, explaining that Mrs Mayers had her own private line, and that she was normally deputised to take all other incoming calls.

That would be one duty which would probably fall to her, Lark recognised as she finished her coffee and nibbled on one of the delicious home-made biscuits.

She had assumed that it had been Mrs Mayers' idea to employ an assistant, but now it seemed as though it must have been her son's. Was that likely to mean that he would be too relieved to hear that his mother had done as he wished to question her past too deeply, or would he be annoyed because his mother had made her final decision without first consulting him?

Either way, there was nothing to be gained from time-wasting speculation. It was almost half-past nine. Time she went downstairs to Mrs Mayers.

The study was unlike any of the other rooms in the house, being far more masculine. Bookshelves lined the walls; velvet curtains hung at the windows; the carpet was Persian and richly coloured, the desk enormous, giving off a scent of beeswax and expensive leather.

'This used to be my son's domain, but when he inherited from his uncle, he decided that he could work just as well from the country as from here,' Mrs Mayers explained. 'It was a difficult time for him. He was just beginning to become established in his career, and the obvious thing to have done would have been to sell or let the Oxfordshire house. I was pleased when he decided to live in it instead, although really it's a family house, and far too large for a single man. Not that he's likely to stay single for ever.'

There was a photograph in a silver frame on the desk: a man in his late fifties with an authoritative face, warmed by a slight smile. There was something almost elusively familiar about him, but Lark told herself she was being over-imaginative.

'My second husband,' Mrs Mayers told her quietly, picking up the frame. 'He died five years ago in a motorway accident. So needless and wasteful.'

There had been so much tragedy in Mrs Mayers' life, she could be forgiven for being so obviously proud of her son. Lark wondered if he was aware of how fortunate he was to be the recipient of so much love.

It soon became clear to Lark as she and Mrs Mayers went through the diaries and files that, over recent months, her new employer had not been able to keep on top of all the paperwork.

'My son suggested a computer, but to be honest I don't think I could cope with one,' she admitted ruefully. 'To be truthful with you, he'd prefer me to retire.' She hesitated a moment and then confided, 'I wasn't very well last winter, and my doctor flapped. Perhaps they're right and I should retire, but I can't. I feel I owe it to my first husband and to our son to carry on for just as long as I can.'

These were sentiments with which Lark could easily identify. Her son must be an unfeeling monster not to realise what he was asking of his mother. This charity work obviously meant so much to her. It even occurred to Lark that he might actually be resentful of the amount of time his mother gave to her first husband and child, but she warned herself it would be foolish to judge him without first meeting him.

At one o'clock they stopped for lunch: a light meal served in a pretty dining-room that overlooked the gardens.

When Lark admired the view, Mrs Mayers laughed. 'Oh, if you like this, wait until you see Abbotsfield. That's the Oxfordshire house. Its gardens are truly beautiful. My second husband proposed to me there.' She smiled reminiscently. 'It was early June and the roses were in bloom—the old-fashioned variety with that lovely musky perfume.' She gave a faint sigh and looked apologetically at Lark.

'My dear, you have the wonderful gift of being a sympathetic listener, and I'm indulging myself shamefully with my reminiscences. I mustn't bore you too much, otherwise you'll run away, and I wouldn't want that. It's such a relief to have someone here who understands how much my work means to me, and who can actually help me with it as well. I confess I have rather been feeling the burden of it these last months, but I haven't dared admit as much.

'One thing that is bothering me is this charity affair.' She frowned, pushing her plate away with her food almost untouched. She *was* worrying about it, Lark realised sympathetically, although she was trying hard not to show it.

'We've got a good number of subscriptions already, but it's the organisation that's causing me problems. My god-daughter Charlotte was going to help me with it. In fact, the whole thing was rather her idea...' Mrs Mayers pulled a wry face. 'I suspect she's found all the organisational detail rather more dull than she anticipated.'

Which, roughly translated, or so Lark suspected, meant that Mrs Mayers been left with a good deal more work to do than she had expected.

'Well, it shouldn't take too long to sort out,' she said consolingly, adding, 'I helped to organise something similar when I was with Thomson Fawcett.'

It was true. The PR company had been asked to organise a charity ball to promote a client's products, and Lark had been heavily involved in that organisation.

'Oh, my dear, you don't know what a relief it is for me to realise how well you and I jell! At first I was afraid...' She broke off and shook her head. 'I've talked far too much about myself. Tell me more about your own life, Lark. Lark...such a pretty name...'

'My parents thought I was going to be a boy. My name came from the fact that the morning I was born my father heard a lark singing outside.'

Lark gave her the explanation matter-of-factly. What had Mrs Mayers been afraid of and why? She must be imagining things, Lark thought, because for a moment it had almost seemed as though someone other than Mrs Mayers had made the decision about employing her, and that was impossible! The older woman was right though, there was a definite rapport between them. Lark had sensed it almost immediately, and that was part of the reason she had been so reticent about taking the job:

her fear that in doing so she might expose a woman she liked rather much to her son's wrath.

But now she had learned of Mrs Mayers' poor health, things had changed. Now nothing on earth would induce her to give up her job, because now she knew that Mrs Mayers genuinely needed her. The state of the files was proof enough of that. Lark had already privately decided that she would put in some extra time in the evening in order to get them sorted out as quickly as possible.

'Oh, by the way, my son will be dining here later in the week, and I would like you to join us, Lark. I want you to meet him.'

Ah, so the inspection had arrived, just as she had anticipated it would! Well, now that she was armed not only with the knowledge of her own honesty, but also Mrs Mayers' need of her, nothing was going to make her abandon her employer. Nothing and no one...certainly not Mrs Mayers' arrogant son, Lark decided. After all, she was used to dealing with arrogant men now. She had cut her eye teeth on the most arrogant man of all—James Wolfe. She doubted that even Mrs Mayers' precious son could exceed James Wolfe's mammoth self-conceit.

She deliberately neglected to let herself remember just exactly how she had dealt with James Wolfe's arrogance in demanding entry to her flat...and...and making love to her...Because that was what that kiss had been.

She shuddered suddenly, and Mrs Mayers looked concerned.

'Are you cold, Lark? Is the heating...?'

'No...No, I'm fine.' She forced herself to smile.

It was time she put James Wolfe completely out of her thoughts.

CHAPTER FOUR

Two days later, Lark had not only restored order to the untidy files, she had also made up a check-list for the charity ball, and started to make inroads into its organisation. Details of the various options open to them with regard to staff, food, music and décor had been meticulously written down and then typed before she had placed them in the folder she had earmarked for Mrs Mayers' attention.

A glance at her watch told her that it was four o'clock. Too late to seek out her employer, who would now be having her afternoon rest—a necessity insisted upon by her doctor.

Lark had also learned that before the charity ball took place Mrs Mayers was hoping to visit Boston, where she was also chairwoman of their branch of the charity.

'I should have gone before Christmas, but I wasn't well enough,' she had admitted to Lark. 'Now, with you with me to take care of everything...' She hadn't said any more, simply smiling affectionately at her new employee, and Lark had responded in kind.

Lark found it difficult to continue with her work; the slightest noise made her jump. The reason she was so tense was that this evening was the evening she was going to meet Mrs Mayers' son.

The whole household seemed to be affected by the promise of his presence, or, in her case, by the threat of it.

And what had surprised Lark a little, probably in view of her own dread of meeting him, was how highly he was regarded by the other members of the household. It was natural, of course, that Mrs Mayers, as his mother, should love him, but Lark had learned from the house keeper in particular that, despite his extremely high-powered career, he still made time to help and advise Mrs Mayers with her charity work, and that it was he who had campaigned tirelessly to secure for the charity the patronage of a top royal.

It had surprised Lark a little to discover how involved, albeit in a very quiet and unobtrusive way, he was with the charity. Somehow or other, initially she had gained the impression that he rather disapproved of his mother's activities. However, the more she worked on the files, the more she noticed the brief, scribbled comments on their pages, often of an extremely helpful and thoughtful nature, and when she mentioned them to Mrs Mayers, they turned out to be made by her son.

'He's like his father,' she had commented fondly. 'A deeply compassionate man who tends to prefer others not to be aware of his sensitivity. In fact, that's why...'

Lark had never learned exactly what Mrs Mayers had been going to say because her employer had broken off abruptly, looking faintly flushed and anxious, and Lark had tactfully not pursued the matter any further, although it did disturb her that a man she had already decided she would dislike should turn out so disconcertingly to have a very compassionate and caring side to his nature. Was she in danger of turning into a woman who hated and mistrusted all men simply because they were men? The thought made her shiver.

The trial and everything leading up to it still gave her nightmares.

Only last night Mrs Mayers had commented gently that she considered Lark to be an intensely loyal person. That had been when she had been drawing Lark out by talking to her about her family background. She had asked then if Lark had any idea exactly why her cousin had spoken and acted as he had.

Lark had hesitated before fibbing that she had not. She suspected that Mrs Mayers guessed that she was withholding something, but the older woman had not pressed her, simply commenting on her loyalty. If only her son might prove to be as understanding and generous as his mother...But Lark knew deep down inside herself that she was hardly likely to find him so.

She tried to concentrate on her self-imposed task of sorting through Mrs Mayers' many address books in order to make a coherent list of possible subscribers for the ball.

Privately there was one point on which she agreed with Mrs Mayers' son, and that was that the workload would be dramatically improved if only Mrs Mayers could bring herself to install a computer.

When Lark had gently touched upon the subject, Mrs Mayers had instantly informed her that she was hopeless with anything in the least mechanical, and that in fact she was terrified of the mere thought of owning a computer. Of course, she had added, if she could be sure that Lark would stay with her and take charge of the machine... Was there definitely no young man in her life? she had probed delicately.

Lark had shaken her head, a little amused by the satisfied expression that had crossed her employer's face.

Perhaps another young woman in her position might have found her job dull, lacking as it did any contact with her peer group, or with anyone, in fact, other than her employer and her small staff, but Lark enjoyed it; she had no desire to socialise, or take the risk of exposing herself to new friendships. Not yet. Maybe later she might feel differently, but right now...

She glanced at her watch to check the time. Mrs Mayers was insisting that she joined her and her son at six-thirty for drinks. There would be a fourth for dinner, Mrs Mayers' god-daughter, who would then be going out to the theatre with her son.

Lark had wondered if there was a match in the offing between them. Mrs Mayers had not said anything to suggest it, but there had been something in her voice when she mentioned her god-daughter and her son that made Lark curious as to their relationship.

There was only one more address book to go through. As she reached for it, it fell off the desk and she had to scramble underneath it to retrieve it. Consequently she was not in a position to see the person walking into the study and closing the door behind them until she had crawled out from under the desk.

'Really, Miss Cummings, I know you've been dreading meeting me, but there's really no need to go to such lengths to avoid doing so.'

She would have recognised his voice anywhere; that smooth, amused drawl that managed to hold the threat of something harder and less yielding beneath its velvet surface.

James Wolfe!

She tried to stand up and had to clutch the edge of the desk for support.

It couldn't be... She was hallucinating. She had got up too quickly, causing a dizzying rush of blood to her head.

Dizzying enough to produce a lifesize, fully fleshed-out phantom?

Hardly.

She stood staring at him, her eyes huge with shock and pain. How could this have happened? *Why* had it happened?

'Dear me... Have I managed to render you speechless? I only wish I had the same effect on other members of your sex.'

He smiled at her, a confident, amused smile that invited her to share his mockery, but Lark was too shocked to do so. His smile vanished and he looked at her sharply, that same look he had given her in court: brutally assessing, stripping away all her defences, looking into her innermost being.

'I take it that my mother didn't warn you of what to expect.'

Like someone watching a dream sequence in which she had no part, Lark was aware of him frowning.

He was wearing a suit very similar to the one he had worn the evening he called at her flat, she recognised as her shock started to fade, her heartbeat slowing down to its normal rate. The jacket was unfastened, and as he moved the fine cotton of his shirt clung to his body. It was fine enough for her to see the dark shadowing of body hair through it.

A most peculiar sensation thrilled through her. Her glance clung treacherously to him, her mind like a mini-computer relaying a hundred different impressions to her.

He came toward her, enclosing her in a wall of musky heat.

To her shock, her body reacted immediately to her awareness of him. Beneath her sweatshirt she could feel her breasts swelling and hardening. She started to tremble, longing for the courage to push past him and rush out of the room.

'I really *did* give you a fright, didn't I?' He didn't sound amused any longer, and had obviously mistaken the cause of her distress.

It seemed impossible to Lark that he should actually be concerned that he might have scared her, and she backed away instinctively as he reached out towards her.

'What is it?' He said the words softly. 'Do I really terrify you so much? There's no need.'

Somehow or other he had taken hold of her wrist. His thumb found its frantically beating pulse and soothed it; or at least she supposed he must have intended to soothe it. Instead, at his rhythmic caress her entire nervous system went into frenzied reaction: her heartbeat doubled, her lungs refused to expand enough to take in the extra air she desperately needed, and her legs seemed to be incapable of supporting her, so weak had they become.

It was the shock—just the shock of discovering that he was Mrs Mayers' precious son, that was all. But why was he holding her wrist like that? Why was he touching her in a way that she knew quite well was far too intimate for their brief acquaintanceship? And, worst of all, why was she allowing him to do so?

The study door opened and Mrs Mayers came in, saying, 'Lark, have you... Oh, James, you've arrived.'

The moment the door opened, Lark had found herself miraculously free, and she stepped back, putting a safe distance between them again.

'Mother, you've been very wicked,' James said in the indolent drawl that was falling all too familiarly on her ears. 'You didn't tell Lark who I was.'

'Oh, dear,' Mrs Mayers looked flustered and uncomfortable. 'Well, James, she's settled in so well... and she was plainly so terrified at the thought of meeting you...' Here she gave Lark an apologetic look. Had she really been so obvious? Lark wondered miserably. How little she still seemed to know herself. She had had no idea that Mrs Mayers had guessed how much she was dreading meeting her son.

It was true, she realised now, that there had been several occasions when Mrs Mayers had tried to draw her out about the trial, but she had always refused to discuss it. No doubt the older woman had been trying to discover how she felt about her son.

'I didn't want to lose her before she'd had a chance to... to meet you properly.'

'Well, Mother mine, you came very close to doing just exactly that. I thought she was going to faint at my feet when she saw me. Not quite the reaction one hopes to get from lovely ladies.'

'Oh, James,' Mrs Mayers exclaimed fondly, 'I'm sure Lark was going to do no such thing.' She turned to Lark. 'I must apologise, my dear. I should have told you who James was, but it's true, I was afraid of losing you. You wouldn't believe how marvellous she's been, James. She's even trying to convert me into having a computer,' she told her son in amusement.

Lark was glad that neither of them required her to make any contribution to the conversation. She was still in shock, still trying to come to terms with the realisation that James Wolfe was Mrs Mayers' son, and, even more terrifying, her discovery that he only had to touch her for all her preconceived ideas about her sexuality and her upbringing to come crashing down around her.

One thing confused her. If she was so susceptible, why had she not discovered this appalling fact before?

'Lark, I came in to tell you that it's time to get changed for dinner. You wouldn't believe it, James,' she told her son, 'Lark would work twenty-four hours a day if I let her, I'm sure of it.'

'My mother has done nothing but sing your praises to me ever since you arrived.'

The smile he gave her made her heart thump dangerously.

'I—I'm sure you'd rather have dinner alone,' she started to say, but Mrs Mayers stopped her.

'Lark, my dear, you are *not* having dinner in your room. We'd both enjoy your company, wouldn't we, James?'

Lark couldn't bring herself to look at him. He couldn't want her to work for his mother; he was smiling at her now, agreeing with every word Mrs Mayers said, but he was going to find some way of getting rid of her; she just knew it.

As she fled upstairs, she heard Mrs Mayers saying reproachfully to her son, 'James, what on earth have you done to the poor child? She seems petrified of you.'

What had he *done*? Didn't his mother realise what he was like in court? Had she never seen him destroy his fellow human beings...slowly and methodically break them down until they were nothing, until they were totally at his mercy?

She only knew one thing now. There was no way she could calmly get changed and then go down and have dinner with James Wolfe sitting at the same table . . . watching her, waiting for the inevitable moment when he would ruthlessly tear her into small pieces.

Oh, he had smiled and watched and listened to his mother's praise of her, but he would never tolerate her working here, never allow her to stay. The miracle was that she had been allowed to arrive here in the first place. Now she knew why he had materialised at her bedsit so oddly that night. But what she didn't know was why he had left without first making sure that she would not accept his mother's offer of a job. How furious he would be if he knew that he was the main reason she had taken the job! She smiled mirthlessly to herself.

Of course, she could see now quite plainly what had happened. Her solicitor had never recommended her for this job. No, it had all been Mrs Mayers' idea. No doubt she had read about the case, known about her through her son's involvement, and, feeling sorry for her, had made it her business to find out as much about her as she could. It was typical of the kind of thing she would do; she was that type of person—compassionate, impulsive, always wanting to help her fellow human beings. The direct opposite of her son, in fact.

Lark was sitting curled up in the windowseat of her bedroom, her face turned towards the view of the garden, but in reality she was oblivious to it when Mrs Mayers knocked quietly and came in.

'Lark, you mustn't feel uncomfortable about meeting James,' she began without preamble. 'The court case was dismissed. It's in the past now.'

'As far as *you're* concerned,' Lark replied huskily. She turned her head and looked at her employer. 'You must see that I can't stay here now. I . . . I'm sure I'm only echoing what J—what your son must have already said to you. He *can't* want me working for you. I know you were trying to be kind. I can understand exactly what happened, and it was very kind of you to go to such trouble to find me and offer me the job, but we both know that your son doesn't approve . . .'

If she had been looking directly at her, Lark would have seen a most curious expression cross her employer's face, but she wasn't. She was staring down at her own hands, willing them not to tremble.

She had been so happy here...so free from the burdens of the court case, and yet all the time she had felt as though she were allowing herself to drift into a false sense of security. At the back of her mind had been the knowledge that Mrs Mayers' son could so easily destroy her new-found serenity, and that had been before she had known exactly who he was.

'I'll pack my things tonight, and leave first thing in the morning.' Lark swallowed the huge lump in her throat. The last thing she wanted now was to burst into tears, but that was exactly what she felt like doing.

'Oh, Lark, do you really hate him so much?'

Lark stared at her, her words only sinking in slowly, and when they had she crimsoned with mortification. How churlish and childish Mrs Mayers must think her!

'No, it isn't that.'

'Then, my dear, what is it? *Why* must you leave? I thought we were getting on so well together, and you must know how much I've already come to rely on you.'

Lark was confused. She had expected Mrs Mayers to agree with her that she ought to leave, not to try and persuade her to stay.

'I...'

'Please think again. If it's James that bothers you, remember we'll be leaving for Boston soon, and he isn't exactly a regular visitor at the best of times.'

Lark quickly picked up on the slightly forlorn note in her employer's voice; she was making her feel extremely guilty, making her feel, in fact, as though she was running away, deserting her almost.

'I don't want to cause trouble between you,' she heard herself saying uncertainly, when she should have been saying that it was impossible for her to stay.

'Trouble?' Mrs Mayers frowned questioningly.

'Yes. Your son . . .' She paused uncertainly, amazed to see Mrs Mayers grimace in wry amusement.

'He does have a name, my dear, and I promise you it won't poison you if you try and say it. He isn't an ogre, you know.'

'He can't want me working for you,' Lark insisted, unable to respond to that.

'Why on earth not?' Mrs Mayers was quite obviously astonished, which confused Lark more than ever. 'If the reason you want to leave is because you think James doesn't approve, it's the silliest reason I ever heard of,' she told Lark roundly. 'I might listen to my son's advice when I think I need it, Lark, but when it comes to making a judgement of character, I'm perfectly capable of coming to my own decisions. And besides,' she hesitated, and then gave a faint sigh, 'Lark, I think I can understand why you feel the way you do, but try not to confuse the barrister with the man. James was only doing his job. He had been retained by the company who employed your cousin. Obviously they wanted to make sure that no one else would feel tempted to copy him. Too many companies are losing too much money through computer fraud. Once James realised . . .'

'Please, I don't want to talk about it,' Lark interrupted her.

She was close to the edge of losing her self-control, of being dragged back into those dark days that she had just begin to think were now genuinely behind her. The memory of the nights she had lain awake, refusing to allow herself to sleep because her dreams were so haunted, shadowed her face. She was aware of her employer's own uncertainty, too wrapped up in her unhappy thoughts to see the faint frown creasing the older woman's forehead.

'Look, Lark, just promise me that you won't do anything hasty . . . that you'll stay with me for at least another month. By that time we'll be in Boston. I promise you, you have nothing to fear from James.'

What could she do? She owed it to Mrs Mayers to give her her word that she would stay with her for at least that short period of time, and so, reluctantly, she did so.

'Please come down and have dinner with us.'

She saw the refusal forming in Lark's eyes and said quietly, 'You can't run away from life for ever, Lark. I discovered that when my husband and son died. If you still want to leave me in a month's time, then I'll have to let you go. We've only known each other a very short time, but already I've become very fond of you. You're so obviously innocent that I can only marvel that the case ever reached court at all.'

'It reached court because no one else seems to share your opinion,' Lark couldn't stop the bitterness from creeping into her voice.

'Lark, you're wrong,' Mrs Mayers protested, and then broke off as both of them heard the grandfather clock strike. 'There isn't time for us to go into this now, but I promise you that, even if James did disapprove of my employing you, he knows as well as I do that the decision is mine.'

Even if he did? Mrs Mayers was trying to be tactful, but Lark knew the truth. There was no 'even' about it. He did disapprove. He must. After the way he had looked at her as he walked into the court room, after the way he had bombarded her with questions designed to totally destroy her, how could he help disapproving of his mother's employment of someone he had believed to be guilty of a major crime, morally if not legally?

But she had given Mrs Mayers her word that she would stay, and so, instead of packing, she showered and changed into the plain black wool dress that was the nearest thing she had to an evening outfit. The neat white collar emphasised the slender length of her throat, the fine wool highlighting, to Lark's eyes, how much weight she had lost. She was still too thin, despite Cora's delicious meals.

Black suited her; it was perfect with her creamy skin and red hair. The dress covered her from head to toe, and yet, when she checked her appearance in the mirror, she frowned to see how very striking she looked; since her teenage days, her appearance had gone against her. Quite early on her aunt had warned her that the male sex nearly always made the wrong assumptions about girls with red hair. When Lark hadn't understood, she had explained more plainly, leaving Lark feeling both bewildered and hurt. Men associated red hair with the kind of girls of whom her aunt did not approve, and it was for that reason that, as a teenager, she had made Lark wear her hair in a very short and unflattering style. It was only when she had gone to university that she had grown it; initially because she had neither the time nor the cash to spare for hairdressers, and then later because she had realised that shoulder-length hair suited her and was more adaptable.

Charlotte Vail, Mrs Mayers' god-daughter, had called to say that she wasn't arriving until after dinner, so that meant there would just be the three of them for the meal.

Lark delayed going down for as long as she could, but then her conscience reminded her of how kind Mrs Mayers had been to her and how frail her health was, and so, putting aside her own feelings, she opened her bedroom door and went downstairs.

Mrs Mayers had already told her they were having pre-dinner drinks in the drawing-room, but she still hovered uncertainly outside the half-open door, reluctant to go inside and confront the reality of James Wolfe again.

She heard Mrs Mayers speaking and held her breath, not wanting to eavesdrop and not wanting to interrupt, either. A second later she was wishing that she had, when she heard Mrs Mayers saying firmly, 'No, James, I don't think you should say anything. The poor child is absolutely terrified of you. Leave it for a little while.'

So she was right. He *had* objected to Mrs Mayers employing her, but his mother was persuading him not to say anything.

Lark's initial reaction was to walk in and give in her notice there and then, but that would hurt Mrs Mayers—someone who had shown her the utmost kindness—and that wouldn't be fair. Besides, Mrs Mayers needed her...genuinely needed her.

She clung desperately to that thought as she walked into the room, deliberately avoiding looking directly at James.

When she did look at him, it came as a shock to realise that he had changed and was now wearing a formal dinner-suit, the fine weight of the trousers making them cling slightly to the muscular strength of his thighs as he stood up in polite acknowledgement of her arrival. He must still have a room here in this house. Did he commute daily from Oxfordshire, or did he have his own accommodation in the city? Probably not, if he maintained a wardrobe here at his mother's.

These and other equally muddled thoughts suppressed a little of her tension. She heard James asking her what she wanted to drink, and must have made some kind of reply, because several minutes later he was handing her a glass of pale liquid which she realised was sherry. An extremely dry and expensive sherry, she realised.

As she reached out to take it from him, his fingers brushed hers. The shocking sensation that ran through her caused her to give an audible gasp; she couldn't bring herself to look at him, already knowing the mocking look that would be in his eyes. Her reaction to him must be some kind of reverse dislike, and it was just her imagination that made her think that there was danger in allowing herself to dwell too deeply on the significance of such sensations.

'And how do you like working for my mother, Miss Cummings?'

The polite, detached question was his way of tormenting her, she was sure of it. She responded disjointedly, hating him for putting her in a position where she was forced to converse with him as though they had never met before, as though she was, in actual fact, a new employee of his mother's whom he had never met before.

'Lark has been most marvellously helpful in getting the ball organised,' Mrs Mayers enthused.

Lark saw James frown. 'I thought Charlotte was going to help you with that.'

He looked very formidable when he frowned, and Lark wasn't surprised to hear the distinctly cajoling note in his mother's voice as she appealed.

'Oh, James, you know what Charlotte's like. I don't think she realised how much work was involved. She means well, but she's very young.'

Lark who had thought his disapproval stemmed from his dislike and distrust of *her* as a substitute for Charlotte, was stunned to hear him saying curtly, 'She's twenty-two, Mother, exactly the same age as Lark, and yet I don't hear you describing Lark as "very young". The trouble with Charlotte is that she's been spoiled...'

'Yes, I'm afraid she has. I suppose it's unavoidable, really. Charlotte's mother died when she was two,' Mrs Mayers explained to Lark. 'Her father dotes on her, but I'm afraid a succession of expensive boarding-schools is not exactly the best background for a child to grow up against. What are you going to see tonight, James? I'm afraid I've forgotten.'

'I don't know. Charlotte arranged everything.'

Lark was glad when it was time to go in for dinner. She put down her sherry untouched.

'Not to your taste, Lark?' James asked her.

She couldn't help flushing. Was there anything that escaped him?

'It's fine,' she told him, tilting her chin and looking directly at him for the first time since she had entered the room. His eyes were really the most amazing colour: silver, and then grey, shifting between light and dark in the space of a handful of seconds, and then back again in a way that was so fascinating that she forgot what she had been saying. He had thick, black lashes, short and stubby, emphasising his masculinity. His eyes lightened as he began to smile, and then she realised how long she had been staring, and she burst into a husky flood of speech that for some reason made his smile deepen.

'Come on, you two,' Mrs Mayers chided them. 'Cora has made a soufflé, and she'll be furious if we keep it waiting.'

Lark had expected to be ignored over dinner, while mother and son conversed, but to her surprise, not only Mrs Mayers but James as well drew her into their conversation. Was he trying to trap her into some kind of verbal indiscretion? she wondered, answering his smalltalk with monosyllables, quickly returning her attention to her plate.

Once she thought she glimpsed the beginnings of anger in his eyes, as though somehow her reluctance to talk to him had annoyed him.

Mrs Mayers was just suggesting that they adjourn to the drawing-room for coffee when her god-daughter arrived.

Charlotte Vail was one of the most beautiful girls Lark had ever seen: petite and dark, with her hair cut in an expensive and immaculate straight bob, her clothes shrieking Knightsbridge, the string of pearls around her slender throat reflecting the creamy glow of her fair skin.

She greeted both her godmother and James effusively, but for Lark she had only a tiny, cold smile, delivered with an air of condescension that made Lark grit her teeth, knowing that she had been quite firmly and deliberately put in her place.

Charlotte Vail had made it extremely clear that she did not consider her godmother's personal assistant to be on the same elevated social plane as herself.

Normally Lark would have been more amused than offended, but because James Wolfe was a party to Charlotte's snub, she discovered that she was flushing with a mixture of anger and humiliation.

If she had resented James's attempts to draw her into the conversation over dinner, that resentment had been nothing compared with what she had to endure when Charlotte deliberately and almost maliciously excluded her by discussing with her godmother and James her wide variety of friends and acquaintances, none of whom, quite naturally, were known to Lark.

The only comment she addressed to Lark was a pseudo-innocent enquiry into her past and how she had come to work for Mrs Mayers. To Lark's surprise, it was James who came to her rescue, saying smoothly that Lark had been personally recommended to his mother.

'Oh, I see. I thought for a moment you must be one of James's good works.'

Lark saw James frown but, before he could speak, Mrs Mayers stood up and said quickly, 'Good heavens, I hadn't realised it was that time! If you don't leave soon, James, you're going to be late. You do still have your key, don't you? Because Lark and I will both be in bed by the time you come back.'

Lark tried not to react to the discovery that she and James Wolfe were sharing the same roof for the night. She was still smarting from Charlotte's crack about 'good works'. For all her air of innocence, she was pretty sure that the other girl had known exactly how insulting she was being. Did she also know Lark's own circumstances? Surely it wasn't ethical for barristers to discuss the personalities involved in their cases, rather in the same way that doctors did not discuss their patients, but she wasn't sure enough of her ground to know exactly what the ethics of the legal world were. She watched as Charlotte kissed Mrs Mayers and then tucked her arm possessively through James's and batted her eyelashes at him.

'You know you're perfectly welcome to spend the night at my place, darling...'

'And have your father come chasing after me with his twelve-bore? I don't think so,' James responded drily.

What exactly was the relationship between them? Lark wondered later, after Mrs Mayers had pleaded tiredness and gone to bed. The older woman had looked tired, worryingly so. She was by no means as well as she liked to pretend. She *did* need her, Lark acknowledged, and Lark herself felt she could hardly repay her kindness by handing in her notice now, even though her instincts urged her to put just as much distance as she could between herself and James Wolfe; always supposing he allowed her to remain working for his mother.

Mrs Mayers had not seemed to have any doubts whatsoever that James had no intention of interfering with her arrangements. Lark wished she could be as sanguine.

She wrestled with the problem for another half an hour; Cora appeared and asked if she would like a pot of coffee before she herself went to bed.

Lark liked the housekeeper, and appreciated the thoughtfulness she had been shown. As soon as she had realised that Lark worked on in the evenings after Mrs Mayers had gone to bed, Cora had started producing a light supper tray, which she normally brought to the study just before she went to bed.

Lark repaid her kindness by returning the tray to the kitchen and washing and putting away everything she had used.

There was absolutely no way she was going to be able to sleep, so she might as well do some work. Ten minutes later, armed with a pot of coffee and some of Cora's home-made gingerbread, Lark sat down behind the desk and started to work.

Some time later she pushed aside the list she was studying in disgust. It was no use trying to deceive herself, she was not concentrating on what she was doing. The clock outside on the stairs had struck the hour twice since she had started to work, and on both occasions she had lifted her head and wondered exactly when James would come back.

Her stomach muscles were already tensed in anticipation of his return; her bones almost brittle with stress. She hadn't touched the gingerbread; she had barely eaten any of her dinner. If she wasn't careful she was going to lose even more weight, and she would begin to look like a bag of bones; she was lucky that her body was small-boned, which meant that she merely looked slightly frail rather than angular, but tonight, contrasting her own shape with Charlotte's, she had been all too conscious of the other girl's almost lush softness. When she had pressed up against James, the softness of her breast had been cushioned against his arm, her action almost a provocative statement of her femininity.

Lark pushed aside her coffee-cup impatiently. It was no good sitting here meekly waiting for the blow to fall, trying to anticipate just what James was going to say or do; she might as well confront him and have done with it.

Inaction had never suited her; impetuous was how her aunt had disparagingly described her, and now that her mind was made up her tension started to evaporate.

If she didn't allow herself to think about James and Charlotte, she might just be able to get some work done, after all.

She was just congratulating herself on succeeding when she heard the sound of a car purring past the study window and then stopping.

Her stomach twisted in tight knots of anticipation and dread, fine shivers of nervous tension drying her mouth and raising the soft hair on her arms. She rubbed them defensively, refusing to allow herself to give in to her emotions.

It was several minutes before she heard James walk into the hall. There was no accompanying feminine set of footsteps, so he must be on his own, she realised.

It was now or never; she could either confront him, and take the consequences, or she could cower away and wait for the blow to fall, every second until it did an agony of tension and dread.

CHAPTER FIVE

LARK was on her feet and across the room before she had even realised she had made a conscious decision.

She opened the door just as James drew level with it. If he was surprised to see her he masked it well, but then he was an expert at disguising his feelings, she acknowledged bitterly, remembering the way he had remained remote and withdrawn all through her ordeal in court, and yet how at the same time she had known how bitterly furious he was when the case was dismissed.

'Still working?'

Had she imagined that sardonic inflection to the question? Not giving herself time to dwell on it, she said curtly, 'I wanted to have a word with you.'

He looked surprised, as well he might, she reflected, recognising too late the almost peremptory way she had framed her request; her curtness was a result of the tension building up inside her, although she hoped that he would not realise it.

She stepped back into the study, anticipating that he would follow her, and then stopped abruptly when she heard him say, 'Not in there, if you don't mind. As I recall, that room only possesses one comfortable chair, and after just spending three hours perched on one of the most uncomfortable seats it has ever been my misfortune to come across, I'd prefer to conduct our—er—discussion in comfort. Not in there,' he added, when Lark turned to walk across to his mother's small sitting-room. 'Every time I walk into Ma's room I'm terrified I'll dislodge one of her treasures.'

It was true that every surface in his mother's room was filled with keepsakes and photographs covering almost every aspect of her life; although there was no photograph of him there, Lark realised.

'This way.'

She flinched as he touched her arm, directing her towards the stairs; so desperate was she to avoid the physical contact that she was half-way up the stairs before she realised she had no idea where she was going.

'Turn left . . . third door along,' James instructed her when she hesitated.

Lark stared at him, and then blurted out, 'But these are bedrooms.'

The smile he gave her made her skin burn scarlet in anger and embarrassment.

'Most of them are,' he agreed drily. 'But that particular door happens to belong to my sitting-room.'

He walked past her as she hesitated, and opened the door, standing back so that she could see inside the room.

It was in darkness, but before he flipped on the light switch she saw the outline of a couple of deep, comfortable-looking chairs and a desk similar to the one downstairs in the study.

'Satisfied?' he mocked, standing to one side so that she could precede him inside.

There was no reason at all why she should feel as though she had been deliberately coaxed into a trap—after all, she was the one who had demanded the confrontation—but as the door closed quietly behind her Lark had an insane impulse to turn and run.

'You're quite safe. I'm no Count Dracula hungry for the blood of young virgins.'

He was taunting her because he had recognised her nervousness, nothing more, but his words made Lark flinch and say huskily, 'If you were, you'd be out of luck. Virgins are a rare commodity these days.'

At university she had quickly realised how out of step with the rest of her peer group her upbringing had made her, and out of self-defence she had learned to conceal her lack of sexual experience behind a wall of pseudo-sophistication. It was that instinctive defensiveness that made her speak now.

She felt James look at her, the quick flick of his intense glance like fire against her skin. 'Oh, I don't know. They're around—provided you know where to find them.'

He was talking about Charlotte, of course. For all the other girl's open sensuality, she came from the sort of background where she would have been pampered and protected all her life; a gift for the man who would eventually be her husband. Like a goose fattened for Christmas, Lark derided mentally. That kind of attitude was as distasteful to her as promiscuity.

She allowed her mouth to twist scornfully as she looked James in the eye and said acidly, 'I thought that kind of thing went out with the Victorians.'

'It's coming in again,' James told her, not at all fazed by her contempt. 'But this time it's not just the male sex who want to be assured of their partner's purity. In fact, I believe there's an agency in London that specialises in supplying the needs of a certain group of extremely wealthy women who can afford their fees. It makes sense, I suppose, on health grounds, if nothing else.'

He heard Lark's shocked gasp and turned to look at her, one eyebrow lifting questioningly.

'Shocked?'

'Disgusted,' Lark told him roundly, adding bitterly, 'You wouldn't say anything like that to Charlotte, but...'

'You're right, I wouldn't,' he agreed blandly, ruthlessly interrupting her. 'But as a matter of fact, it was Charlotte who told me.'

Lark was stupefied. She couldn't think of anything to say.

'Are you always so naïve that you take everything in life at face value?'

'Why shouldn't I?' Lark demanded, firing up instantly. 'I suppose you think that because I...because of what happened to Gary——' She was trembling now, wrought up both by anger and shock; the years of her aunt's harsh control of her personality were slipping away as nature reasserted itself. 'I suppose you think that because I slept with my cousin... because I blackmailed him into stealing from his company, I'm intimately aware of every vice that exists, is that it?' she demanded.

'Not necessarily.' The mild response stopped her in her tracks. 'Besides, you claimed that you and your cousin weren't lovers, and that you weren't responsible for the thefts—remember?'

'But you didn't believe me, did you?' Lark countered. She was literally trembling with the intensity of her feelings. She had forgotten that she had promised herself that she would be cool and controlled; that she would argue logically and clinically as he had done in court; that she would not lose her temper or her self-control. 'And that's why you want to get rid of me, isn't it? Because you don't believe I'm a fit person to work for your mother. I'll bet you just can't wait to get me out of here. I'll bet you're just dying to throw me out on to the street, because that's where you think I belong... There or in prison. Well, believe me, I'd like to oblige you. In fact, there's nothing I'd like more than to walk out of here right now, because that way I'd never have to set eyes on you again, but I can't.'

She stopped to take a shaky breath of air, dismayed to realise how overwrought she was. Tears weren't far away; she could feel them burning behind her eyes, clogging her throat. She wanted to shout and cry; she wanted to pummel her fists against that broad, unfeeling chest and to make him feel what he was doing to her, what he had done to her with his savage cross-examination. But she could only stand there, shivering, fighting for self-control as she finished hoarsely, 'Your mother needs me. I can understand how furious you must be that I'm here, but no matter what you think of me, I promise you this,' she lifted her head and looked bravely at him, 'your mother is the kindest, most com-

passionate person I've ever met, and rather than hurt
her I'd...'

'Put up with my unwanted presence?'

She stared at him, her impassioned outburst halted by
his wry interjection.

'I agree with you. At least, as far as your description
of my mother is concerned. I also agree with you that
she needs you, and in fact, if you'd allowed me to speak
first, I was going to tell you as much. My mother isn't
well. She needs someone she can rely on. She seems to
have found that someone in you. Like you, I don't want
to upset her.'

His quiet, calm words, so directly in contrast to her
own, maddened her. How did he always manage to get
the better of her?

'It's called experience,' he told her, reading the angry
question in her eyes. 'And besides, it's what I've been
trained to do. I think we should call a truce. Forget the
past.'

Lark blinked, too astounded to make any comment.

'I think we should also talk about getting my mother
a computer. She tells me you've been working every
evening since you arrived. I've been on at her for some
time to get one, but she hates the idea.'

It was all too much for her. She had spent the whole
evening since he arrived bolstering up her courage, trying
to anticipate what he would do, trying to prepare herself
for the fact that he was bound to find a way of making
her leave; and to hear him say calmly and casually that
he felt they should call a truce, that he wasn't going to
even attempt to make her leave, was so much an anti-
climax that instead of being relieved she was intensely
angry.

How dared he let her get herself worked up like that
and then calmly dismiss the whole subject with one brief
sentence? Did he imagine she was as cold and emo-
tionless as he must be himself? Did he think she could
simply switch off and start discussing computers, when

she had spent the last five or six hours imagining that the happiest days she had known in a very, very long time were about to be brought to an abrupt end?

She wanted to launch herself at him and claw that calm, superior look from his face; she wanted to see him raw and bleeding the way she was bleeding inside, but instead all she could do was stand there and shiver while huge tears filled her eyes and rolled down her face. She knew she should turn away, hide herself from him, but she simply couldn't move.

She heard him call her name, but it was a distant sound, barely penetrating her anguish.

'Lark.'

He said it again, and this time she tried to focus on him, but his image was too blurred, shifting rapidly, and then oddly obliterated by the stark whiteness of his shirt.

'Oh, my God, Lark. Come on, now. It's all right. It's all right.'

She was aware of the words being spoken, of being lifted, carried, held against something warm and comforting while she wept silent, agonised tears for all that she had endured.

A hand touched her hair, stroking it away from her face, its partner gently caressing her back. Against her breast she could feel a steady, comforting thump. Instinctively she burrowed deeper into the warmth surrounding her, protecting her; she was still shivering in bursts of violent but silent tremors that made the man holding her frown and curse himself with equal violence, while he kept on murmuring soft words of comfort and wondering how long he was going to be able to hang on to his self-control.

Gradually the tears stopped; gradually the tremors subsided and Lark returned to normal.

It was a shock to find herself in James's arms, lying against him as he sat in one of the armchairs. Her face was pressed against something warm and damp, and it was several seconds before she realised it was his throat and that it was damp because she had been crying, and then only because her tears ran down his skin and on to her own. She tasted them uncertainly with her tongue, her mind confused and fogged by the intensity of what she had experienced.

James felt her tongue brush his throat and froze, unable to believe that she had actually touched him. He looked down into her eyes and saw that they were huge and dazed, and realised that she had no awareness at all of the provocation she was offering.

If he had any sense at all he would get up right now and take her to her own room.

He shifted her weight slightly in his arms and saw her frown slightly, her tongue tip searching her lips as though it missed the contact with his flesh. Without further thought, his head bent, his mouth capturing her tongue tip.

Heat shot through her like sheets of fierce sensation— no, like pulsing waves that washed higher and higher, Lark thought bemusedly. She was having the most delicious dream, full of physical sensations so intense and so unfamiliar that she couldn't do anything other than concentrate on the wonder of them.

And then the bubble burst. She heard James speaking to her, urgently and angrily; she felt the bite of his fingers in the soft flesh of her upper arms and the dream was destroyed. She focused on him and realised in shock that he was far too close. She could feel the warmth of his breath against her mouth, her whole body seemed to be throbbing with a strange urgency.

'Lark . . .'

What was he saying to her? What did it matter? What mattered was that she had to get away from him. She shouldn't be here with him like this. In fact, she couldn't understand how she came to be in his arms at all.

She started to struggle, filled with panic and shock. Immediately James let her go.

So suddenly, in fact, that she almost fell on to the floor, and would have done so if his hands hadn't restrained her, but the moment she regained her balance she pushed him away, standing up on legs that trembled.

'Lark...'

'Don't come near me.'

Her voice trembled almost as much as her legs.

'Very well. But don't forget, will you, Lark, that you've promised you'll stay with my mother? And I wouldn't try breaking that promise if I were you,' he threatened her softly.

In the morning, Lark couldn't believe that she had actually gone to bed and immediately fallen asleep after what had happened. She hadn't even dreamed, or at least, not dreams which she could remember. Emotional exhaustion, a more detached part of her brain told her, but even that made her wince and almost cower back under the bedclothes.

How could she have behaved the way she had? How could she have actually cried all over James Wolfe then clung to him like a lost child?

It was the shock, she excused herself; the shock of discovering that she had put herself through hell, and all for nothing. He had never intended to make her leave; he actually wanted her to stay...

Because his mother needed her.

What did it matter why? she asked herself impatiently, trying to dismiss her idiotic need to believe that he had actually somehow come to realise that she was innocent and that he had been wrong.

A man like James Wolfe would never admit to being wrong; it wasn't in his nature. He was cold and remote.

And then she remembered the way he had kissed her, and this time there was nothing to blur her awareness or to hide behind.

And she had kissed him back. She actually remembered winding her arms around his neck. She could still feel the softness of his hair against her fingers.

She made a sharp sound of distress and buried her hot face in her pillow. How on earth was she ever going to be able to face him?

She had abandoned herself to him like a . . . like a . . .

She sat bolt upright in bed as someone knocked on her door.

Dear God, please don't let this be him. She didn't think she could bear it.

And yet, when the door opened and Cora came in, carrying a breakfast tray, her first feeling was one of almost sharp disappointment.

'James said you were up last night working. Still at it when he came in. He said to let you have a lie in this morning, and for you to have your breakfast in bed.'

'Oh, no!' Lark was appalled, as much by what the housekeeper must be thinking of her as by her own mixed reaction of guilt and shock. And James's instructions were so out of character, his concern for her so at odds with the kind of man she knew him to be . . . Or thought she knew him to be.

It was odd how easily the doubt slipped into her mind; almost as though, at heart, she wanted to believe that he had another side to him.

In a panic, she dismissed her truant thoughts and said, 'But Mrs Mayers will be expecting me downstairs . . .'

'Not yet. She's resting today, so you needn't rush. Oh, and James said to tell you that he's arranging for someone to come and see you about a computer.'

'He's . . . he's gone, then? James . . . I mean, Mr Wolfe? Why is his surname different from Mrs Mayers?' Lark added impetuously, flushing a little at the look the housekeeper gave her.

'Well, Mrs Mayers has always used her first husband's name for her charity work. Mrs Mayers-Wolfe she is really, but hardly anyone uses her full name, and of course James uses his own father's surname. Sometimes it causes a bit of confusion,' she added. 'He's a barrister, you know,' she told Lark chattily, apparently unaware of Lark's sudden pallor and tension. 'Works far too hard too, just like his mother; forever worrying about folks who don't deserve to be worried about,' she added darkly. 'Now, mind you eat all your breakfast,' she warned Lark, as she opened the door.

Breakfast in bed. She was being spoilt, and on James's instructions.

Oh, God, what on earth must he be thinking of her, weeping all over him like that? It was so unlike her; she hadn't even cried when her parents were killed. Her aunt had said that she mustn't. She never cried, never behaved as she had done last night. She shivered, remembered how she had let James comfort her, blindly reassured by the sound of his voice, and most of all from simply being close to him. But why? He was her enemy. She hated him.

It was like suddenly discovering that the ground beneath her feet, far from being solid and safe, was extremely dangerous; it was like straying into quicksand and then being too terrified to move in case one became trapped in it.

But trapped in what exactly?

Hurriedly, Lark poured herself a cup of coffee. She had wasted too much time on James Wolfe; she wasn't going to waste any more.

The representative from the computer company arrived after lunch. A pretty girl a couple of years older than Lark, she quickly and simply explained to both Lark and Mrs Mayers how much easier the new equipment would make their working lives.

Mrs Mayers refused to be convinced. If she agreed to allow the equipment inside the house, then Lark would have to take full responsibility for it, she announced firmly.

Lark hesitated, knowing quite well that if she went ahead and ordered the equipment she was going to have to stay with Mrs Mayers for far longer than a month. Before last night, that wouldn't have bothered her at all, quite the reverse. But now... Despite the truce they had agreed, she wasn't at all confident that she was going to be able to cope with the knowledge that James Wolfe had the right to more or less walk in and out of her life whenever he chose.

How ironic that was, when one of her reasons for taking the job in the first place had been her fear that he might try to pursue her!

And yet, despite that, she found herself agreeing that the equipment should be installed on a trial basis.

'The work could be done while we're in Boston,' Mrs Mayers suggested. She turned to Lark. 'I forgot to tell you, we're going to have to leave for Boston almost immediately. Lark, an old friend of mine, a co-trustee of the charity's funds, has had a heart attack and is in hospital. Would it cause you any problems if we left tomorrow?'

'None,' Lark assured her promptly. If anything, it would be a relief to get away. In Boston it would be far easier to put James out of her thoughts.

She went to the front door with the computer salesgirl, who promised to get everything organised as quickly as she could.

'By the way, did you see James when he came in last night?' Mrs Mayers asked her when she went back.

'Only briefly. Charlotte...Miss Vail is very pretty, isn't she?' she asked, desperately trying to change the subject. Why was it that the mere mention of James's name was enough to make her start trembling with nervousness?

'Very... but I'm afraid, as James says, she's also very spoiled. Her mother and I were very close friends. I think Charlotte will improve when she marries. She needs someone older to take charge of her... keep a firm hand on her, so to speak. Oh, dear, that sounds dreadful, doesn't it? But Charlotte has never made any secret of the fact that she wants to get married. She has no ambitions to be a career girl at all.'

Not only did Charlotte know she wanted to get married, she also had her future husband picked out as well, Lark suspected. Her pride wouldn't allow her to question her employer on the exact nature of the relationship between her son and her god-daughter, but it sickened her to think that James had come straight from Charlotte to her. That kiss might even have been meant for the other girl, a girl whom he considered too innocent to subject to the fierce male desire Lark had sensed. What would have happened if she hadn't come to her senses in time?

Oh, come on, she derided herself, you know what would have happened. He would have taken you to bed and made love to you.

There it was, out in the open at last, that desire she had seen blazing from his eyes so briefly in the court room.

And the worst of it was that she herself wasn't immune to it. If she had been... She closed her eyes, not wanting to allow her thought to go any further.

'Lark, are you all right?'

She opened them again and smiled reassuringly. 'Fine... If we're going to Boston, oughtn't I to start making some arrangements?'

Luckily Lark had a current passport which she had obtained while she was at university. The travel agent listed in one of Mrs Mayers' many address books was able to provide them with tickets on a British Airways flight that left at lunch time the next day. The flight was a long one, almost eight hours, but because of the time difference they would arrive in Boston in the afternoon.

Lark had known that Mrs Mayers had a home outside Boston, but what she had not realised was that she also kept a full-time staff there as well.

'We'll ring Hennessy and arrange for him to pick us up. It's quite a long drive out to Marble Head, well over an hour. And then we'd better speak to Mrs Hennessy as well. She'll want to know how long we're staying. You'd better tell her at least a couple of weeks. Oh, and Lark, you might tell her that I doubt that we'll be doing much entertaining. I want to spend as much time as I can with Jack, and there will be quite a lot of work to get through as well.'

Lark didn't mind. Work was exactly what she needed right now. It was the only way she had of keeping James out of her thoughts. She made the transatlantic call herself and heard for the first time what was soon going to become the familiar Boston twang.

Mrs Hennessy sounded as calm and efficient as her British counterpart, and Lark suspected that Mrs Mayers had that rare gift of inspiring genuine respect and affection among those who worked for her.

'Pack summer-weight clothes,' Mrs Mayers warned her when they eventually sat down to dinner. 'I know it's still cool over here, but in Boston it will be much warmer. You will need a jacket of some kind, though. We're right on the coast, and the breeze can be pretty sharp at night.'

Mrs Mayers had made a personal phone call to the hospital to check up on her friend. He was still in intensive care, she told Lark, but responding well to treatment.

'I'd like to go to see him as soon as we arrive. Hennessy can take us to the house and then take me back to the hospital. And then you must have at least a couple of days off, Lark. The house is rather isolated, I'm afraid, but if you wish, Hennessy could take you into Boston. I'll have to try to organise something while we're over there so that you can meet some other young people.'

'I'm going to Boston with you to work,' Lark reminded her gently. 'Please don't worry about me. You've got enough to think about.'

'You're such a kind girl, Lark, but you mustn't be too selfless. You're far too young to spend all your time with an old lady like me. When we get back, I must ask Charlotte to introduce you to some of her friends.'

'Oh, no, it's kind of you, but really it isn't necessary.' Lark was caught between dismay at the thought of being thrust into the kind of social circle Charlotte Vail obviously inhabited, and amusement at the thought of the other girl's reaction to her godmother's desire for her to mix socially with one of her employees.

'I'm really quite happy just as things are,' she added, feeling that some explanation for her hasty denial was required.

'Maybe, but you mustn't shut yourself away from the rest of the world, Lark. I know how easy it is to do so. I fell into the same trap after my first husband died, but, emotionally, women aren't designed to be alone. We need to be involved, nurtured.' Lark suspected that the modern career woman would not agree with Mrs Mayers' observations, and yet Lark was beginning to realise that the older woman was far more shrewd than she sometimes allowed people to think.

After dinner, Lark went up to her room to pack. It didn't take very long.

Lightweight clothes, Mrs Mayers had said. She looked grimly at the contents of her wardrobe. Apart from jeans and T-shirts, all she owned that fitted that description were a couple of inexpensive dresses bought when she was at university. Telling herself that it didn't really matter if she wasn't Charlotte Vail with a wardrobe full of expensive clothes to choose from, she lifted them out of the wardrobe.

There were certain papers that Mrs Mayers wanted to take with her and, once she had finished her packing, Lark went downstairs to get them. While she was in the study the telephone extension bell rang. She picked it up without thinking, giving the number and her name.

'Still working, Lark? I hope my mother is paying you overtime.'

Lark tensed at the sound of James's voice, her fingers gripping the receiver.

'I understand you managed to persuade my mother to at least give the computer equipment a try.'

With every word her tension increased. She was beginning to feel dizzy. She wanted to hang up on him and blot out the sound of his voice, but she was an employee working for his mother and her business training would not allow her to do so.

Abruptly the tone of his voice changed.

'Lark, about last night...' Her hand felt sticky with nervous perspiration. She started to shake and she was sure she would have dropped the receiver, business training or not, if Mrs Mayers hadn't unexpectedly walked into the room.

Instead she thrust the receiver towards her, and said huskily, 'It's James, your son. I...'

She fled from the room before she could betray herself completely. It wasn't until she was upstairs that she realised how idiotically she was behaving. What on earth would Mrs Mayers think of her?

Lark could only hope that she would put her odd behaviour down to her dread that James might decide to dismiss her. She wondered if James had already told his mother about their truce, and from there it was only one logical and very short step to asking herself why, when she no longer need fear that she would be dismissed, she should start shaking with that mixture of apprehension and excitement that was unique to her exchanges with James.

Emotions—fear, such as the fear she had experienced in court—couldn't simply be put on one side just because their perpetrator told her that they could. Yes, that was it, she decided thankfully. It was fear that made

her react the way she did. Fear? She didn't like the
question mark her conscience hung over the word, niggling at her until she was forced to admit that the thrill
of sensation that ran through her every time she spoke
to James or saw him had not had its roots in fear.

So she was not indifferent to the man. What did that
prove, for heaven's sake? she questioned herself impatiently. Nothing, nothing at all, other than the fact
that she was as vulnerable as the rest of her sex to the
power of sexual magnetism. It was just unfortunate that
in her case that magnetism should be generated by a man
she should more properly detest.

When she realised that she had come upstairs without
Mrs Mayers' papers, she went back to the study. Mrs
Mayers was still there. She looked rather confused.

'Lark, did James say he wanted to speak to me? He
seemed rather angry that you'd gone. I think he must
have wanted to discuss the computer with you,' she added
vaguely. 'Anyway, I told him that he'd have to wait now
until we get back. I think he's a little worried that I might
change my mind, and he probably wanted to enlist your
support.' She gave Lark a wry smile. 'It seems that,
whatever your other differences might be, you and my
son are united in your determination to drag me into the
computer age.'

'Only because we know that ultimately it will lessen
your workload,' Lark assured her. Here, at least, she
was on safe ground, and so she spent a good ten minutes
earnestly averring her belief that the new technology
would be of tremendous assistance to her employer.

'Only as long as you're here to operate it, my dear,'
Mrs Mayers told her frankly. 'And I said as much to
James. I told him that I'd warned you there was no point
in either of you expecting me to master the monster's
intricacies, and I also told him that you'd promised me
that you wouldn't leave if it was installed.'

Lark had been sorting through some papers, but she
looked up at the triumphant sound in Mrs Mayers' voice.

'You look tired,' Mrs Mayers told her. 'No working late tonight, Lark. I think James is beginning to suspect me of being a slave-driver. He told me this morning that you were still working when he came in last night.'

'Only because I couldn't sleep,' Lark defended.

'You should be spending your evenings dancing, not working. Forgive me if I'm prying, Lark, but your cousin—were you in love with him?'

Lark shook her head and said honestly, 'No. Oh, I know that the papers tried to suggest that we were more than just cousins.' She stumbled a little over the words, remembering her shock and bitter disgust at the thinly veiled suggestions in many of the newspapers that she and Gary were lovers.

'Was he in love with you?'

Again Lark shook her head, slightly more forcefully this time.

'No—if anything, we disliked one another.'

'So there was no woman in his life,' Mrs Mayers mused. 'Strange, one would have thought from his behaviour that there was.' She saw Lark's face pale and exclaimed apologetically, 'Oh, my dear, I'm sorry. I shouldn't pry like this. Do forgive me.'

'It's not that,' Lark told her shakily, unable to explain that her shock had been caused by how close Mrs Mayers had come to guessing the truth. If she could see it so easily, then why could no one else? she wondered a little bitterly. Why was it that Mrs Mayers was so easily able to believe her innocence, while her son could only see her as guilty? What did it matter what James thought about her? she asked herself fretfully, as she gathered up her papers and gripped them together.

'We'll need the minutes from the last meeting over here,' Mrs Mayers started to say, and then checked as she saw the neatly typed list that Lark was holding.

'Oh, dear,' she said ruefully, 'you've already got them, haven't you? I'm sorry, Lark. I'm so used to my own inefficiency.'

'You aren't inefficient,' Lark told her firmly. 'It's just that paperwork isn't your forte.'

She was surprised by the vigour of Mrs Mayers' laughter.

'My dear, you do have the most delightful and tactful way of putting things,' she exclaimed when she had finished laughing. 'You're also a treasure of an assistant. While I know that you're wasting your talents working here for me, I can't help feeling glad that my son...'

She broke off in some confusion, and Lark felt quick sympathy for her. No doubt she had been about to say that she was glad that James was allowing her to stay in his mother's employment, but had realised that to admit that he did have the power to veto her decisions would not be tactful.

Lark had only flown on a couple of occasions before; once on a brief weekend visit to Paris with a group of fellow students, when they had been crammed on board a charter flight, which had proved to be a most uncomfortable experience. The other occasion had been a family holiday with her aunt and uncle and cousin early in her teens.

Neither occasion had prepared her for the luxury and efficiency of first-class travel. When Mrs Mayers had realised how little luggage Lark was taking with her, she had been delighted.

'I keep a wardrobe of clothes in Marble Head, and that's all you're taking. We shan't have anything to check in at all.'

She proved to be quite correct. Lark was told that her one small case could be classified as hand luggage and go into the first-class cabin with her.

After their tickets had been checked, they were told that they could proceed to the Concorde Lounge to await the announcement for their flight. The lounge was a revelation to Lark; a world apart from the bustle and turmoil of the usual departures lounge.

Here soft carpets hushed the sound of footsteps. Passengers relaxed in comfortable chairs discreetly placed around small tables. The smell of freshly brewing coffee filtered temptingly around the room. The uniformed steward dispensed glasses of champagne and soft drinks in addition to a tempting array of light snacks.

Lark watched in amazement as other arrivals went up to the counter and helped themselves to whatever they wanted.

'It's all part of the service,' Mrs Mayers told her in amusement, watching her round-eyed disbelief.

Lark flushed, mumbling that Mrs Mayers must find her very naïve.

'Not at all,' she was reassured. 'In fact, it makes me appreciate just how very fortunate I am. After a while one tends to take all this for granted, which is wrong, really. Come and sit down and we'll have a cup of coffee, or would you prefer champagne?'

Lark shook her head. She had no head for alcohol at all and, besides, she remembered reading somewhere that it was the very worst thing one could drink on a long flight. In almost no time at all, or so it seemed, they were told that they could now board the plane.

Again the luxury and space of the first-class cabin amazed Lark. There was room to spare to stretch out her legs in front of her. An attentive steward took Mrs Mayers' coat and hung it away in a small closet. Lark felt she had scarcely time to take in her surroundings and fasten her seat-belt before they were actually taking off.

She had brought a book with her to read, but there was so much to fascinate her that she found she had not even opened it when the steward announced that he would be coming round with lunch menus.

Mrs Mayers, who had been lying with her eyes closed, opened them when she heard this announcement.

'Lunch, excellent! Isn't it amazing how hungry one gets when travelling?'

It was, Lark acknowledged, and the menu only increased her appetite.

'The meals on this flight are normally excellent,' Mrs Mayers promised, 'although James complains they aren't substantial enough. I'm afraid he's a true Englishman where his food is concerned. He adores roast beef and stodgy puddings.'

Visualising James's lean, athletic body, Lark found this difficult to believe. Seeing her expression, Mrs Mayers chuckled.

'He enjoys them, but he doesn't live on them.'

After lunch they watched a film. Half-way through it Lark fell asleep, and the next thing she knew, Mrs Mayers was shaking her gently to warn her that they would soon be landing.

Lark felt guilty. She should have been the one taking care of her employer, not the other way around.

They were practically the first people off the plane and, because neither of them had any luggage to collect, they were soon through to Immigration, where they had to separate since Mrs Mayers had retained her American nationality.

Lark tensed a little under the careful scrutiny of the Customs official, but within a very short space of time she was free to join Mrs Mayers on the other side of the barrier.

'Larry should be waiting for us outside with the car,' Mrs Mayers told her. 'You'll soon discover that here in America, everyone uses Christian names.'

Although Mrs Mayers had warned her that it would be warmer in Boston, Lark wasn't prepared for the wall of heat that hit her as they walked out of the air-conditioned coolness of the airport building. It was like being wrapped in a hot, wet blanket, and she almost staggered under the force of it.

Mrs Mayers laughed, but not unkindly. 'It does come as rather a shock, doesn't it? But don't worry, you'll soon get acclimatised. We have full air-conditioning at the Marble Head house. Ah, good, there's Larry now. Come along, this way.'

Mutely Lark followed her to the large, black limousine with its darkened windows, her eyes widening a little in amazement as she studied it.

'Hideous, isn't it?' Mrs Mayers exclaimed, wrinkling her nose. 'James normally absolutely refuses to ride in it. He says it makes him feel like somebody in the Mafia.'

Lark could see his point, and it was an impression that was reinforced by the uniformed chauffeur who got out of the driver's side of the car. He was tall and swarthily complexioned, with dark hair, but when he smiled the menacing impression of his features was banished. He greeted Mrs Mayers so warmly that Lark chided herself for her over-active imagination.

'Drive through Boston, will you, Larry?' Mrs Mayers instructed him as he closed the car doors beside him. 'This is Lark's first visit, and I'd like her to see something of the city.' She'd already introduced them, and now Lark saw the chauffeur smiling warmly at her in the driver's mirror as he obeyed Mrs Mayers' instruction.

'Luckily we're too early for the rush-hour traffic. It gets pretty hectic around here, I'm afraid. Boston has boomed in recent years, especially as a new financial centre. You'll find new skyscraper blocks going up all over the city. I've heard that some of the developers are even trying to tear down blocks in the old Back Bay area. Not a very popular move with the more conservative members of Boston society. Most of their families owned properties there at one time or another,' Mrs Mayers informed Lark. 'Back Bay was the area to live in the city at one time, but now most people prefer to live out in the suburbs.'

As they drove through the city, the chauffeur pointed out several buildings to her, but Lark, muggy from the heat and jet-lagged, could hardly take in what she was being told, and only had a fleeting impression of a busy but not overcrowded city where the cars seemed huge in comparison to their British counterparts and the people in the streets were dressed in lightweight summer clothing that made her feel acutely conscious of the heaviness of her own suit.

'Don't worry, you'll be able to take more in next time,' Mrs Mayers told her.

They were travelling north along the coast, and every now and again Lark glimpsed signposts with familiar names: Manchester, Gloucester—familiar and yet unfamiliar. And if she felt alien, how must those first lonely settlers have felt? No wonder they had given their new land names from their old homes.

'We're in commuter country now,' Mrs Mayers informed her, 'and these houses are typical of New England.'

Lark looked at the pretty buildings, their exteriors clad in what looked like white wooden panelling. She noticed the area gradually becoming more hilly. Marble Head was right on the coast, and it had got its name from the fact that British sailors, seeing sun strike on the cliff face, thought that it was made of marble. Although most of the small villages along the coast were inhabited by Bostonians, many of them still retained their original pioneer flavour, and in some the houses had been passed down from generation to generation.

They were travelling along a more minor road now, green lawns stretching away to either side of them, framing impressive mansions. Lark didn't need to be told that this was a very upmarket and expensive area. The houses grew more and more impressive, until at last they could no longer be seen from the road, shielded from the eyes of curious passers-by by hedges and, in some cases, high walls.

They were still climbing, and to her right Lark caught the occasional glimpse of the ocean. When looking at it, she suffered her first surge of homesickness. What time was it in England? What was James doing now?

She caught herself half-way through the treacherous thought.

'Are you all right? Don't worry. We'll soon be there,' Mrs Mayers assured her kindly, mistaking the reason for her small, indrawn breath. 'It's only another mile or so.'

It was, but what she had neglected to tell Lark was that almost all of that mile or so of road ran adjacent to the boundary of her own property; a fact which Lark wasn't to discover for several days. As it was, she was marvelling the immaculate state of the almost-English hedge to her right, when suddenly the car came to a halt outside a pair of very impressive wrought-iron gates.

They opened as though by magic, and they drove in between them, down a long, gravelled drive towards a house of weathered, dark grey stone. 'This house was built by one of my first husband's ancestors early in the 1800s, some say with the fortunes he had made in dealing in arms during the Revolution.' She broke off and turned to the chauffeur. 'Thank you, Larry; neither of us has any luggage to speak of, but perhaps you'd go and tell Mary that we've arrived, as I'm sure Lark would like something to eat and drink. I'm afraid then I'll have to ask you to take me back to Boston almost immediately, but I want to check with the hospital first. Oh, and perhaps you'd ask Mary to show Lark her room. I'll go straight to mine and freshen up a little.'

Larry waited until both of them were out of the car before disappearing in the direction of the back of the house.

The front of the house faced towards the road, the back towards the sea, but Lark's view of the Atlantic was shrouded by the mass of shrubbery that separated the front of the house from the back. The exterior design of the house resembled a mini-fortress, a resemblance which was intensified by the huge oak door.

'I suspect my husband's ancestor entertained fantasies of baronial splendour,' Mrs Mayers told Lark with a chuckle, as she pushed the door open. 'The original plans actually contain a provision for a moat. Luckily, this promontory here is solid rock, and so he was forced to abandon that idea. Come on inside.'

The hall was oval, its walls painted Wedgwood blue, the mouldings picked out in soft off-white. The floor was tiled in marble, a staircase curling up one side towards the upper storey, and as she looked up, Lark could see the domed ceiling right above them, and realised that the light pouring into the hallway came from the stained-glass windows.

'An improvement added by a Victorian ancestor,' Mrs Mayers told her, following her glance. 'I've instructed Mary to prepare you a bedroom overlooking the ocean. I thought you'd like that, but if you'd prefer to change...'

Lark shook her head. 'No, that sounds absolutely lovely.' She was conscious of feeling grubby and rather tired, and also of the fact that Mrs Mayers must be anxious to go to see her friend. 'I'll go and unpack,' she told her. 'You'll want to make an early start in the morning, I expect. If you could tell me where the study is, I could perhaps go in there and check through the files while you're out.'

Mrs Mayers smiled affectionately at her. 'Lark, you're a glutton for punishment! I'm not going to tell you where the study is because I don't want you to work this afternoon. This is your first experience of a long transatlantic flight. If you'll take my advice, you'll simply familiarise yourself with the house and garden this afternoon, and then have an early night. If you like, I could get Mary to give you a mild sleeping tablet. I find that the best way to avoid jet-lag is to immediately adapt to the hours of the country I'm in, but that isn't always as easy as it sounds.'

'No, I think I'll be all right,' Lark told her, shaking her head, not liking the thought of taking any drug unnecessarily.

'Well, if you have any difficulty at all in sleeping, don't hesitate to give Mary a ring. Now, I'd better get up to my own room and make myself presentable,' Mrs Mayers said briskly. 'Ah, here's Mary.'

She smiled as a pretty, brown-haired woman hurried into the hall. Mary was nothing like Mrs Mayers' house-keeper in London. She was younger, for one thing, and despite her Boston accent Lark immediately recognised her Irish heritage. She had the true Celtic colouring, the pale skin and deep blue eyes surrounded by thick, smudgy lashes. Her face dimpled when she smiled, and she was prettily plump in a way that fine-boned women often could be, with delicate ankles and wrists.

'Mary, would you take Lark up to her room?' Mrs Mayers asked when she had introduced them. 'She's tired out, poor girl, although she will try to deny it and pretend she wants to start work.'

Mary clucked sympathetically. 'That transatlantic flight's a killer, isn't it? We went to visit my family in Ireland last year, and it took me nearly a week to get back on my feet again. If you'll come this way,' she said to Lark. 'You're on the second floor.'

The second floor, Lark discovered, was not the top storey of the building, but what at home would have been described as the first floor. She realised that she was going to run into some confusion with the language, and hoped that everyone would be as patient and under-standing as Mary was.

Her room, although very different from the one she occupied in the London house, was every bit as com-fortable. The furniture was Victorian, its heaviness lightened by the pretty wallpaper and curtains. She was delighted to discover that it had a balcony, and that from her window she could see right over the garden to the cliff edge, and then across to the ocean itself.

'We have private access to the beach, down those steps over there,' Mary told her, nodding in the direction of the beginning of a pathway at the top of the cliff which Lark could only just see. 'When you look out at that ocean, it's hard to believe there's anything out there but water, isn't it?' Mary commented.

'England's there,' Lark said softly, looking out across the grey vastness of the Atlantic.

'Homesick?' Mary questioned her, not unkindly. 'My grandmother came out from Ireland when she was seventeen. I remember her telling me how much she missed her home when she first came here, and how she would stand and look out across the ocean.'

'But she settled here eventually?' Lark asked.

Mary chuckled. 'Oh, yes, indeed, once she had met my grandfather. Mrs Mayers said you didn't bring much luggage, but if you've anything you want me to unpack...'

Lark shook her head. 'No.'

'Your bathroom's through here,' Mary told her, pushing open a door, 'and Mrs Mayers' bedroom and sitting-room is three doors down the corridor. If you like, I can bring you a tray of tea up here, or if you prefer, you can have it in the kitchen with me.'

Lark quickly opted for the latter. She didn't really want to be on her own, and Mary seemed friendly. It made her realise how long it was since she had actually talked to a member of her own sex, apart from Mrs Mayers. At home she had been wary of conversation, dreading being questioned about the court case, but here she felt no such inhibitions. After all, it was scarcely likely that her notoriety would have crossed the Atlantic ahead of her!

She waited until she had seen Larry driving away with Mrs Mayers before going down to the kitchen. Thanks to Mary's directions, she found it easily enough. It was a large, sunny room at the back of the house. She and Larry had their own accommodation, a complete flat above what had originally been the stable block, Mary told her as she made the tea.

'It's a bit big for us now that our kids are at school,' she told Lark, explaining that their two sons were away at boarding-school. 'It's mostly private schools round here, and neither of them would have felt comfortable mixing with kids from such wealthy backgrounds, so we decided it was better to send them away.'

Lark sympathised with her, sensing that she missed her sons. They chatted for a while, mainly discussing Mrs Mayers' involvement in her charity work, and then, when Lark started to yawn, Mary stood up and said firmly, 'If I were you, I'd go to bed. You'll feel the benefit of it in the morning.'

Wise advice, Lark reflected as she made her way to her bedroom. She wanted to explore her new surroundings, but she felt too exhausted to do so. She wondered ruefully what it was that Mrs Mayers possessed that enabled her to make the long journey back to the city, while she, who was so much younger, could do nothing but crawl into bed in a state of almost complete exhaustion.

She slept well and dreamlessly, and was woken by Mary at seven o'clock when she came in with a tray of tea.

When Lark protested that she was not here to be waited on, Mary shook her head. 'There's no problem. I'm always up early. I don't normally take anything in to Mrs Mayers until half-past eight, and then she gets up shortly after nine.'

That gave her ample time to go downstairs and familiarise herself with the layout of the study, Lark reflected, drinking her tea.

The house was cooler than she was used to, but she had already ceased to notice the hum of the air-conditioning. Mary had told her how to find the study, and she made her way there as soon as she was dressed.

At ten o'clock, when Mrs Mayers joined her, she had already made a thorough investigation of the files, and had been relieved to discover that they were not in quite as bad a state as those in England.

'Right, down to work,' Mrs Mayers announced cheerfully. 'I rang all the other committee members last night and we're having a meeting in Boston at noon. I want you to come with me, Lark, so that I can introduce you to them, and then I'll take you on a quick tour of the city. You may want to do some shopping,' she added tactfully, eyeing the thin wool sweater and heavyweight skirt that Lark was wearing.

Lark flushed a little, not wanting to explain to her employer the paucity of her summer wardrobe and its unsuitability for her present duties.

'Oh, and that reminds me,' Mrs Mayers added, producing an envelope, 'as we're over here, I'll pay your salary in American currency. I've drawn some money out of the bank, and here's a small advance for you.'

From the thickness of the envelope, there was quite a considerable amount of money inside it. Lark took it reluctantly.

'How was your friend?' she enquired.

'Much, much better than I had expected. Out of intensive care now, in fact, and demanding to be allowed to go home. Not that the hospital is going to let him, but it was good to hear him complaining, nevertheless.'

Lark envied Mrs Mayers her thin silk suit when they eventually set out for Boston a little later. She herself was still wearing her sweater and skirt and, despite the air-conditioned interior of the car, her sweater was beginning to stick clammily to her skin.

'We are lunching with the other committee members at the Ritz Carlton, one of Boston's most prestigious hotels,' Mrs Mayers informed her. 'It's on Newbury Street,' she added with a twinkle in her eye, 'one of the best shopping areas in the city. If we have time, we'll do a little window shopping after lunch.'

Lark quailed a little at the thought of lunching in one of Boston's smartest hotels wearing her woolly sweater and skirt, but there was nothing she could do about it, and besides, she wasn't there to socialise, she reminded herself. She was there to work.

This time, as they drove through Boston, she was able to take in more of her surroundings. The hotel was opposite the city's main park. The concierge obviously recognised Mrs Mayers, and welcomed her in to the hotel. They were lunching in a private dining-room, Lark discovered.

The Ritz was patronised in the main by old Boston and visiting Europeans, Mrs Mayers told Lark as they went upstairs in the lift. That probably explained the faintly French Empire décor, Lark decided, responding with a smile to the liftman's cheerful, 'Have a nice day.'

They were the last to arrive, and the only women. Of the eight men who stood up as they entered the room, only one could have been described as young. He was tall, thin and almost gangly, with smooth, soft, brown hair and sunburnt skin. His smile was friendly, if a little diffident, Lark reflected as Mrs Mayers introduced her to him.

'Lark, this is Hunter Cabot, one of the mainstays of our small organisation. I'm afraid he inherited us from his grandfather, who was one of our most generous supporters.' She smiled warmly at Hunter before introducing Lark to the other members of the group.

They were all, in the main, businessmen who gave their time and expertise free of charge to the charity, and that in itself was an indication of Mrs Mayers' persuasive powers, Lark suspected.

She was amused and a little envious to realise that all of them were a little in love with her employer, in the most gentlemanly way, of course. She enquired after their wives and families, chatting to them with a warmth and sincerity that Lark had recognised at their first meeting.

There were the minutes of the last meeting to be gone through, and items on the agenda to be discussed. Mrs Mayers wanted to talk to them about her plans for the charity ball in England. They had done very well in the previous financial year, one of the committee members told them, raising a substantial sum to go towards the medical research being conducted at John Hopkins.

'Money well spent,' another one said, standing up and smiling at Mrs Mayers. Lark remembered that she had been introduced to him as one of the specialists working on the research.

'We've now got to the stage where we can isolate the chromosome disorder which gives rise to the imbalance. The next stage will be to discover how we can determine whether that disorder has occurred in the growing foetus, and for that, I'm afraid, we need more money.'

Various suggestions were put forward on ways and means to raise such money. Lark diligently noted them all down in her best shorthand. The time flew so quickly that she was surprised when Mrs Mayers announced that they should adjourn for lunch.

As they sipped pre-lunch drinks, the table was cleared and relaid with gleaming silverware and starched linen. A centrepiece of roses was placed on the table, their perfume filling the air.

Over the leisurely lunch, Lark observed again how very skilled her employer was in dealing with other people. At three o'clock, she announced that she and Lark would have to leave as they had shopping to do.

Outside in the sunshine, Lark was once again very conscious of the difference in temperature between London and Boston. She felt terribly uncomfortable in her too-warm clothes and, as though she was aware of this, Mrs Mayers set off briskly in the direction of what she explained to Lark was an excellent store. No doubt it was, Lark recognised, boggling a little as she saw the famous name of Bonwit Teller up on the doorway.

In no time at all they were whisked upwards to the fashion departments, and Mrs Mayers had organised a bemused Lark into trying on a selection of pretty summer casuals. It was no use protesting that she didn't need them or that they were too expensive. Mrs Mayers was determined to have her own way, Lark realised, emerging from the changing-room at her employer's insistence to parade the outfits for her inspection.

They were lovely pastel skirts with flattering pleats that swung frivolously against her legs. Toning T-shirts in softest cotton, and lightweight tops in matching prints. Somehow or other she found herself agreeing that both the turquoise and the pink were so perfect for her colouring that she couldn't possibly not buy them.

They made suspiciously little impact on the wad of dollar bills in her envelope. Just how many months' wages was Mrs Mayers actually advancing her? Lark wondered wryly, as she handed over the cash and accepted the purchases.

'Now a dress,' Mrs Mayers announced firmly, 'but not from here. I know just the place.'

Just the place turned out to be a very small and exclusive shop selling French and Italian fashions. Several dresses were produced for their inspection, but Mrs Mayers shook her head until she saw the drift of cornflower-blue silk over the assistant's arm.

'The colour is right,' she announced decisively. 'Let's see it on.'

Lark protested that an evening dress, because that was exactly what it was, was something she was never likely to wear, and therefore a needless expense.

'Nonsense,' Mrs Mayers told her. 'Of course you'll wear it, probably when Hunter takes you out.'

Lark goggled at her.

'He hasn't asked me out,' she protested.

'Not yet, maybe, but he will,' Mrs Mayers assured her. 'I saw the way he was looking at you over lunch. Poor Hunter, he'd love to get married and have a family, but he's very shy and conservative. I keep telling him that an English wife is just what he needs.'

Lark wondered if her employer was actually trying to matchmake. If so, she was surely doomed to failure. No man as conservative as she claimed Hunter Cabot was would ever consider marrying a woman with her kind of past.

'Try the dress on,' Mrs Mayers instructed her firmly, and Lark had little option other than to accede.

Of course, the dress fitted perfectly, almost as though it had been made for her. It had a brief bodice with tiny shoestring straps, the shell of the dress moulding her waist and hips, and finishing just on her knee. Sheer panels of cornflower-blue silk flared out from the waistline, whispering seductively when she walked.

'Ravishing,' Mrs Mayers pronounced when she came out of the fitting-room. 'That colour is perfect for you. I knew it would be.'

There seemed to be no question that Lark was going to buy the dress, but she demurred when Mrs Mayers asked the assistant if there were shoes to match.

'Please,' she protested in an agonised whisper, 'the dress is so expensive, I don't even know if I can afford that, never mind shoes as well.'

'I'm sorry, my dear. I'm bullying you, aren't I?' Mrs Mayers apologised with a smile. 'That dress is so perfect for you, you must have it. Look, why don't you let me buy it for you?'

Lark was horrified, and she was also in a very difficult position. She really had no option other than to take the dress and to insist on paying for it herself. She counted out the dollar bills with apprehension, pleased to discover that there was still a good quantity left. She had no idea exactly how long they would be staying in Boston, and she didn't want to spend all her money on the first day.

It was well after four o'clock when they finally left the shop.

'I think we'll have afternoon tea at the Ritz, and then back to the house,' Mrs Mayers suggested.

They got back at seven o'clock and, after an early dinner, Lark settled down to work. There were documents to be prepared in connection with the lunch-time meeting, and several lists of ideas Mrs Mayers had had consequent to the lunch.

The telephone in the study rang at ten o'clock. Lark picked it up automatically, and was surprised to hear an American male voice asking for her. It turned out to belong to Hunter Cabot, who was ringing to ask rather diffidently if she would like him to show her something of the area.

'I know Mrs Mayers will be tied up with business for the next few days. I'm afraid I'm here to work, not to enjoy myself,' Lark interrupted him. But Mrs Mayers, who was sitting at the other side of the desk, shook her head and mimed to Lark to hand her the receiver. Reluctantly, Lark did so.

'Hunter, my dear,' she heard her employer exclaim, 'of course Lark is free to go out with you. Tomorrow? Yes, of course.'

She replaced the receiver with a smile. 'Hunter will call for you at ten o'clock in the morning, Lark.' She gave her a mischievous look. 'You'll find he's extremely well informed about the Cape Iron area. I expect he'll take you to the yacht club for lunch.'

'But Mrs Mayers, I'm here to work,' Lark protested, to no avail.

Her employer simply smiled and bent her head back over the papers she had been studying before saying calmly, 'Lark, my child, the world won't come to an end simply because you have a few hours off.'

Although she had not expected to do so, Lark found that she enjoyed Hunter's company. When he forgot about being self-conscious, he was an interesting companion and, as Mrs Mayers had promised her, he was very informative about the area, as well he might be. His family had lived there for many generations.

Mrs Mayers had already told her that he was an extremely wealthy man, but he seemed almost frightened of giving that impression, Lark realised as she listened to him.

Did he think she might latch on to the fact that he was wealthy, and pretend an interest in him, purely for that reason? She felt mildly sorry for him. He was a very diffident man, lacking in self-confidence, and yet he wasn't unattractive. He needed a woman who was kind and motherly to boost his self-confidence. As he showed her around the small village of Rockwell, she learnt that, like her, he had been orphaned young. He had been brought up by a grandfather who sounded as though he had been extremely remote, which probably accounted for his shyness, Lark reflected.

He didn't work, having no need to do so, which explained why he was free to devote the whole day to her in the middle of a working week. But, even though Lark liked him, when he eventually drove her back to Mrs Mayers' home and paused hesitantly before asking her if she would have dinner with him the following night, she had to fight against an instinctive impulse to refuse.

What was the matter with her? This was her chance to put the past behind her and start living a more normal life. Why was she so reluctant to go out with Hunter? It wouldn't have anything to do with the fact that he wasn't James, would it?

CHAPTER SIX

'ARE you sure you don't mind me having the evening off?' Lark asked Mrs Mayers anxiously.

It wasn't the first time she had asked the same question, and her employer looked wryly at her and told her, 'Lark, I'm quite sure that Hunter would be less than flattered if he could hear you. Of course I don't mind, my dear. It will be the first evening you've had off since you started working for me. Where are you dining? Do you know?'

'The Bostonian, I think.'

Mrs Mayers' mouth twitched slightly. 'An excellent choice. Hunter obviously wants to show you off. Everyone who's anyone in Boston dines there,' she explained to Lark. 'What are you going to wear?'

There was only one thing she could wear—the new dress she had bought in Boston.

She prepared for her dinner date with reluctance, a reluctance she was hard put to it to give a name to. After all, it was not as though she was leaving Mrs Mayers alone for the evening; her employer had announced that she was dining with friends.

When had the peace and tranquillity she had expected to find in Boston, with the width of the Atlantic between herself and James, turned to dullness and boredom? When had she first begun to realise that she was mentally drawing comparisons between Hunter and James to the former's disadvantage? Hunter was a nice man: kind, thoughtful, the kind of man whom she felt she could trust to believe in her implicitly, and yet compared with James...

But why should he be compared with James? What was she doing even thinking about James in the first place?

She tugged agitatedly at the zipper on her dress, and stepped in front of the mirror to study her reflection. It looked every bit as good on as it had done in the shop; the rich blue fabric flattered her colouring, the misty panels of her skirt floating out around her in the chill of the air-conditioning, while beneath them the pencil slim sheath of the underdress hugged her body.

The upper swell of her breasts was just visible above the provocatively cut neckline—discreetly, so Mrs Mayers had assured her when she had first tried the dress on. Now she was not so sure. The few hours she had spent sunbathing had given her skin a peachy glow, and she touched the slight swell of flesh uncertainly.

As Mrs Mayers had already pointed out, Hunter was very conservative. If he was indeed taking her to the Bostonian to show her off, he might prefer her to wear something a little more discreet, but what? This was the only evening dress she possessed.

Outside she heard a car coming up the drive. It was too late to start worrying about her appearance now. Hunter had arrived.

She picked up the jacket Mrs Mayers had insisted on lending her, letting her fingertips luxuriate in the soft pure mohair before she slipped it on. The off-white wool was a striking contrast to the richness of the cornflower-blue silk.

Mrs Mayers came out of her room as Lark reached the top of the stairs.

'You look lovely,' she told Lark approvingly.

'You don't think...' Lark touched her neckline irresolutely. 'I don't want to offend Hunter.'

Mrs Mayers laughed. 'My dear, no man worthy of the name would be offended by the way you look tonight. Far from it. If I were you, I'd worry more about making sure that Hunter brings you straight home,' she added forthrightly, causing Lark to flush slightly.

Hunter was wearing a dinner suit. It suited his lanky frame, adding breadth to his shoulders.

'Don't keep her out too late,' Mrs Mayers warned him as she waved them off. 'She's got to work tomorrow.'

Lark recognised the Bostonian Hotel from her brief tour of the city. It was set on the edge of the old market area, and going up the outside of the building in the glass lift with Hunter she was able to look down on the prettily illuminated area below them.

The restaurant was very busy, but the *maître d'* bustled forward when Hunter gave his name, smiling welcomingly at them before showing them to a table for two.

As he pulled out the chair for her to sit down, Lark was conscious of the glances of other diners, and was glad that she had taken Mrs Mayers' advice about her dress.

Without exception, the women around her were elegantly and expensively dressed, hair and nails gleaming with the gloss of expert care and the kind of life-style that allowed them the time and money to be able to pamper themselves. Unlike her, she reflected wryly, glancing at her own short, unpolished nails that only shone with their own healthy pink gleam.

A window ran the entire length of the restaurant, giving an impressive view of the city skyline.

A waiter brought menus and asked if they wanted a pre-dinner drink.

Lark refused, and Hunter, she noticed, asked only for spa water.

As she studied the menu, she listened to snatches of conversation, fascinated by the brief glimpses it afforded into other people's lives.

'This place is Boston's top restaurant,' Hunter told Lark importantly. 'The food here is the best in the city.'

Privately, Lark had preferred the European elegance of the restaurant at the Ritz Carlton where Mrs Mayers had held the meeting and taken her after their day in the city, but she was too tactful to say as much to Hunter, who so obviously wanted her to be impressed.

The menu was in French, with vaguely *nouvelle cuisine* undertones. They both ordered and, while they waited for their first course to arrive, Hunter started to talk about his work for the charity.

This was the first time Lark had ever actually talked to a man under thirty who was so wealthy that he did not actually work for a living.

For all his inherited wealth, Hunter was no playboy type, intent on filling his time with a rich man's amusements. He obviously took his work for the several charities with which he was involved seriously, and yet Lark could not help contrasting his life-style with that of James.

Hunter, pleasant though he was, was a mere shadow when compared to the substance and male energy that was James.

She heard Hunter say something about a boat, and realised that he was inviting her out on it. Hastily she reminded him that she was in Boston to work, softening her refusal with a promise that she would check with Mrs Mayers to see how busy they were going to be.

After dinner, Hunter asked her if she would like to go on to a club. Lark shook her head. She had enjoyed the evening in a mild sort of way, but she had no desire to prolong it.

Hunter drove her straight home, hesitating only momentarily when it became obvious that Lark wasn't going to invite him in.

He made no attempt to touch her or to kiss her, and she wasn't quite sure how she would have reacted if he had.

It was still only quite early, a little after half-past ten; Americans didn't like dining late. Mrs Mayers was still out, it was the Hennessys' night off, and she felt far too wide awake to even think of going to bed.

Instead she unlocked the terrace door and stared down the flight of stone steps that led to the beach. The sea had always fascinated her, and now, with the ocean's vastness clothed in darkness, the sound it made as it caressed the rock face was pleasurably soothing.

At the bottom of the steps she slipped off her high heels, her toes curling as they felt the cool rasp of the sand. There was enough light for her to see the cream heads on the breakers as they rolled in.

She sat down on a boulder, watching them, almost mesmerised by their movement, trying to count them to see if it was true that a seventh wave was always higher, and then losing count as she became absorbed by the sheer power.

Perhaps that was why, when she first saw the male figure emerging from the ocean, she could only sit and stare, transfixed like some latter-day Greek maiden confronting the human form of the sea-god Poseidon.

As he strode through the foam, he pushed his hands through his wet hair, sending silver droplets cascading over his shoulders and torso.

Fascinated, she observed the powerful play of his muscles, fluid and sleek, each movement co-ordinated and sure.

He came out of the water and shock coursed through her as Lark realised that he was naked.

She stood up hurriedly, dislodging a small shower of stones, and realised her folly. He turned his head, and she knew that he had seen her.

She couldn't breathe; there was a painful constriction in her chest, a tightness that wasn't quite a pain, and that had something to do with the quick, shallow beat of her heart.

He was coming towards her. She wanted to turn and run, but she couldn't, the boulder was in her way. Instead she averted her head, praying that the darkness would cover the scorching blush suffusing her skin.

Unlike her, he didn't seem to be the slightest bit embarrassed by his nudity. Where she would have cowered away, tried to hide herself, he seemed totally unconcerned, proud almost.

'Good evening, Lark.'

She had known, of course, exactly who it was right from the start, but she refused to look at him, refused to acknowledge the amusement in his voice as he made the formal greeting. If only her heartbeat would slow down to normal, she might be able to ask him exactly what he was doing here... Although, of course, he did have every right to be here; it was his mother's home, after all.

She could almost feel his presence now; the delicate nerve-endings under her skin quivered with her awareness of him, every muscle in her body strained under her determination not to turn her head and look at him.

'What are you looking at?'

He was standing beside her; she could actually feel the warmth of his breath against her skin. A droplet of sea water fell on to her exposed shoulder and she flinched, turning on him angrily, willing herself to look only into his eyes and nowhere else.

'I'm not looking at anything,' she told him pointedly, furious to see the laughter glinting in his eyes.

'How indignant you look,' he drawled softly. 'Surely not because of me...'

His arrogance increased her anger.

'I'm more than indignant,' she told him roundly, 'or didn't it occur to you that I might find it embarrassing to discover a nude man down here on the beach?'

'Well, the thought did occur to me,' he agreed blandly, 'but then you looked at me for so long, I decided to ignore it.'

'I did not look at you,' Lark denied, horrified as much by the tell-tale burning of her skin as by anything else. The moonlight was such that she was probably even more clearly revealed to him than he was to her. She put a protective hand against the top of her dress, wondering anxiously if he had also noticed the betraying hardening of her nipples and how they had pushed against the soft bodice of her dress. Hardly from all that distance, surely?

'Oh, but you did,' James corrected her softly.

His hand caught her face, turning it so that it was impossible for her to avoid his gaze. She watched tensely as his eyes changed from the same silver as the ocean to nearly black.

'And I enjoyed it,' he told her meaningfully, making the blood run hot through her veins. 'When my mother's family first bought this land, they owned the salvage rights to the coast here, did she tell you that? Everything they found on the beach belonged to them, to do with exactly as they wished. Do you know what I'd like to do with you, Lark?'

Amazingly, she couldn't speak, couldn't demand that he stopped whispering such tempting, appalling words in her ear, that he stopped touching her skin with those light, tormenting movements of his hands that were robbing her of any ability to think coherently.

As though her silence was somehow acquiescence, he continued softly, 'I'd like to take off your clothes and lie you down in the surf and make love to you until neither of us could hear the sound of the ocean for the song in our blood—until you were deaf, dumb and blind to anything else. I wanted you the moment I saw you, and it's got worse, not better. I've left a desk full of files to come over here to be with you. I once thought that only teenagers did things like that. I've even lost weight. Feel...'

Lark moaned in protest as he took her hands and placed them on his flesh.

How hot it felt, still damp from the sea, grainy with sand and salt. She had no idea what kind of game he was trying to play with her, no idea what he was trying to prove.

She looked up at him to tell him so, and saw the fierce, burning need glittering in his eyes and she was lost.

Her body arched into his as though by instinct, her arms locking round his neck, her silk dress crumpled between them as he caught hold of her.

'James!'

'Don't say anything,' he told her thickly, bending his head. 'Just kiss me.'

It was an appeal her senses couldn't resist.

Her lips parted and trembled as she hesitated slightly. She felt the heat of James's breath against her mouth and then within it.

This was no tentative, explorative kiss exchanged between two people who were strangers to one another, Lark realised, the last of her resistance evaporating like sea foam in the sunlight, her whole body quickening against him. His flesh burned as though it were on fire, the male, musky scent of him making her head swim. He was fully aroused, his body hard and demanding against her own, his hands gripping her hips and then clenching in the soft flesh of her bottom as he tried to find relief from his need.

No one had touched her like this before, aroused her like this before. Lark had only her instincts to listen to and to follow, her body, already soft and pliant, moulded itself eagerly to James's touch, her breasts pushing resentfully against the barrier that separated her from his flesh.

His tongue thrust into her mouth, mimicking the fierce movements of his body. Lark cried out in aching response, a soft mewling sound almost lost beneath his kiss. She lifted her hand to tug at the shoulder-strap of her dress where it had slipped and was biting into her arm, and almost instantly James fumbled for her zipper, tugging it downwards with fierce, uncoordinated movements that matched his erratic breathing.

A soft glimmer of light bathed her skin as James put enough distance between them to remove her dress. He hadn't released the zipper properly, and the fabric bunched round her hips. James kneeled on the sand beside her, cursing softly as he tried to remove it.

Lark bent to help him, the fabric falling in a soft puddle at her feet.

James made a sound deep in his throat, something between triumph and despair. He was still kneeling in the sand and, as she looked down at him, he slid his hands along her thighs, splaying his fingers possessively across her hips, stroking the narrow curve of her waist, making her shiver with need and pleasure, before finally cupping the pale roundness of her breasts.

She saw him look at her and felt her nipples tighten sharply, the ache inside her body intensifying. Unable to move, unable to draw her gaze away from the sight of James kneeling at her feet in an attitude of almost pagan male adoration of her body, at the same time she was herself intensely aware of his masculinity and power, albeit a power that for the moment was tamed and leashed by his desire for her. His fingers spread out across her pale breast, so dark and exciting, drawing from her such sensations as they stroked and caressed and then cupped her flesh; simply drinking in the sight of her aroused femininity.

He touched his tongue tip to the dark areola of her nipple, drawing circles of fire against her flesh that made her shudder and arch. Small, hoarse sounds strangled in her throat as she fought against the twin surges of sensation and shock that flooded her unprotected nervous system.

Nothing in her life had prepared her for this: for this pleasure that was almost a pain, for this pagan responsiveness to a man's touch, for this sensitivity of her own flesh.

Her fingers curled into the solid muscle of James's shoulders, initially surely to push him away, to stop the flames destroying her flesh, but, as though James read another message in her clenched grip, his tongue stroked the jutting peak of her breast. When she looked down at herself, she saw that her flesh was bathed not only in the mysterious light of the night sky, but also in the moistness of James's mouth.

He was looking at her, too. A dark, hungry look, tightening his face, pushing his flesh back against his bones so that all she could see was his face's maleness, his eyes almost the same colour as the ocean where the moonlight silvered its spray.

She lifted her hand from his shoulder and touched his face, tracing his profile, caught up in an ancient mysticism too powerful for her to deny.

He shuddered beneath her touch, stopping her when her exploring fingers began to trace soft patterns against the tiny flat discs of his own nipples, pushing her hands behind her back and holding them there.

'Oh, God, Lark . . .'

How anguished he sounded! She felt an instinctive urge to comfort him, to ease his distress. She tugged against the imprisoning band of his fingers, and instantly he released her wrists, but before she could touch him she felt the shock of his fingers playing against her bottom beneath the thin fabric of her briefs, his mouth hot against her skin as he tugged impatiently at the final barrier of delicate fabric.

Lark had no thought of stopping him. Tiny pulses of excitement and need quivered eagerly through her as she stepped free of her briefs. She expected James to stand up and take her in his arms, but instead she felt the shocking drag of his open mouth against her flesh, searing the sensitive skin of her thigh, burning the tender swell of her stomach, his tongue probing the tiny indentation there, making her clutch at his arms to prevent herself from collapsing as her legs turned boneless and fluid.

Dimly she recognised the intensity of his need, and that recognition sent a fine thrill of sensation quivering over her skin, sensitising it almost unbearably to the

fierce pressure of his mouth as it slid over the soft swell
of her breast and then fastened on her nipple, drawing
it into the hot, moist cavern that was waiting to pleasure
it, stroking, sucking, teasing, tasting her until she was
crying softly caught up in a tumult of emotion she had
not known existed, holding his head against her body,
offering herself to him as her body arched responsively
against his mouth.

Her response drove him over the edge of his self-
control; he had promised himself it wasn't going to be
like this, but he was beyond rational thought, beyond
anything other than the sensation of her tender flesh in
his mouth, her soft cries of pleasure. He raked his teeth
against her nipple, and Lark tensed as she felt a corre-
sponding thrill of sensation begin deep inside her body.

James felt it, too.

His hands stroked, moulded and caressed her, his
mouth still drawing shivers of delight from her as he
enjoyed the thrusting eagerness of her breasts, and then
finally his hand slid between the quivering softness of
her thighs, touching her delicately, so that her body
opened out to him.

He took hold of her hand and brought it to his own
flesh, letting her feel how much he wanted her, and then
he placed her gently on the sand, and entered her with
such skill and delicacy that she barely felt the sharp flash
of pain that made her catch her breath and tense her
body for the briefest space of time before it died away
to make way for the waves of sensation aroused by his
quickening thrusts, his body totally unable to withstand
the allure of the hot, tight embrace of hers.

It started slowly, just the merest frisson of sensation,
growing and gathering momentum, inciting her to score
her nails against James's flesh and to arch her back in
an ecstasy of sensation that made her cry out and writhe
helplessly against him, until he showed her how to match
his own rhythm, imposing it on her as she fought against
its dominance, before realising that it was enhancing

every tiny spasm of pleasure, until they became an unending spiral that went on and on, engulfing her, drowning her, and finally abandoning her on some far away, unfamiliar place, with the weight of James's body pressing her to the sand, and the sound of his harsh cry of release still ringing in her ears.

He let her lie until her breathing had returned to normal, and then said quietly, 'I think we'd better go back to the house, before another nocturnal stroller finds us.'

He got up and helped Lark to her feet, passing her her clothes.

She felt desperately weak and shaky, tears smarting behind her eyes, an awful feeling of desolation creeping over her.

She felt James touch her eyelashes and then the corner of her eyes, and knew that his fingertips would be damp.

'A classic case of post-coital blues,' he told her softly. 'Unfortunately, there's nothing I can do about them down here on the beach.'

He saw her start to shake and cursed. God, he should have had the sense to wait at least until they were in the privacy of his own rooms before making love to her. But he hadn't been able to wait, that was the truth of the matter.

Lark was struggling with her dress.

'Here, let me.' James turned her round gently, and slid up the zipper with much more ease and expertise than when he had slid it down.

Which only went to prove how true it was that a man in the throes of passion...

'You go up. I'll follow you in a few minutes...'

Of course. He would hardly want to be seen with her. The Hennessys might be back, or worse still, his mother. Lark didn't even know how long they had been down here on the beach, and of course he wouldn't want anyone to know what they had been doing.

James saw her face and said quietly, 'You're wrong. It's just that I have to get dressed, and you're shivering already. A mixture of cold and shock, I suspect.'

'Shock?'

His eyes darkened, and Lark quivered beneath the look he gave her.

'It isn't every day that a woman loses her virginity.'

The breath hissed out of her lungs. She hadn't even thought he'd noticed.

'You knew,' she said stupidly.

She saw his mouth curl in the beginning of a smile.

'Oh, yes, my little innocent, I knew. Now go back to the house and get warm before you freeze to death. I shan't be long.'

The house was just as empty as it had been when she left it. She wandered into the kitchen and started to make some coffee. Her hands trembled and she felt another surge of tears prickle behind her eyes.

Post-coital blues. James would know, of course. She wasn't the first woman he had made love to. She almost dropped the coffee at the fierce stab of jealousy that attacked her. The mere thought of James touching another woman as he had touched her was like a physical pain inside her.

She put down the coffee jar and leaned against the worktop.

Why bother to try and hide from the truth any more? She was jealous because she loved him.

Her senses accepted the accusation so easily that she knew it was true; even her body had known it was true, she acknowledged despairingly. It was only her silly, idiotic brain that had fought against the knowledge, denying it, not wanting to admit that she could actually have been so foolish.

There was a notepad and pen attached to the counter, and quickly she scribbled a message on it. She couldn't face James again tonight. Not now. Everything had happened so quickly; their lovemaking had been so intense, so overwhelming, that there had been no room for anything else, but now...

Just for good measure, she bolted the door to her room. She put in her note that she wanted to be left alone. She waited tensely for several minutes, anticipating that James would ignore her message, and then she heard the sound of a car, and realised that they were no longer alone.

He wouldn't come to her now, and she was shocked to discover that the knowledge did not entirely please her. She must be cautious and careful; she was no child, to read what did not exist into a man's momentary physical desire. James was probably already planning exactly what he would say to her to make it clear to her that he was not emotionally involved. It was only her pride that stopped her from crying out loud at the thought. The same pride that helped her to live through the ordeal of Gary's accusation.

How could she ever have even imagined that James might have any emotional feelings for her? How could he, when he believed her guilty? No, to him she was just a desirable body, nothing more.

Eventually, she fell into an exhausted sleep.

CHAPTER SEVEN

'WELL, my dear, did you enjoy yourself last night?'

Lark couldn't help it, she started nervously, a guilty flush darkening her skin, her glance straying helplessly across the table to James as she struggled to answer his mother's question. And then she realised that Mrs Mayers was referring to her date with Hunter.

Her flush deepened, scalding her, and she gave a visible shudder.

'Oh, dear, not as bad as that, surely?' Mrs Mayers was openly amused. 'Poor Hunter, he will be disappointed.'

'Hunter?' James enquired lightly, lifting his head from the paper he was reading, and subjecting Lark's flushed face to cool assessment. 'Are we talking about that paragon of gentlemanly conduct, Hunter Cabot?'

'Yes, James, we are, and there's no need to take that tone. Hunter is a very nice man.'

'If you say so, Mother.' He gave Lark a narrow-eyed stare. 'Is that what you think, Lark? That Hunter is very nice?'

Lark didn't know what to say. It had been a shock to come downstairs to find him in the breakfast-room. Mrs Mayers had smiled at her when she saw her hesitating on the threshold, calling her in and exclaiming in a pleased voice, 'Isn't this a lovely surprise, Lark? James has taken a few days off. He arrived last night after you'd gone to bed.'

Lark hadn't been able to look at him. How clever of him to cover himself like that, but it hadn't been necessary; she had had no intention of referring to what had happened between them.

126

'James, really, whatever Lark thinks of Hunter is no business of yours. Good heavens, is that the time? Lark, I don't want to rush you, my dear, but I'd like to be in Boston for eleven. I've got a meeting at noon, and I'll need you to take notes.'

'Are you going in to Boston? I'll cadge a lift in with you, if I may. What are you doing for lunch?'

'I'm eating with the other members of the committee, unfortunately,' Mrs Mayers replied regretfully.

'Well, maybe Lark will have lunch with me instead, then,' James suggested.

Lark could hardly believe her ears. She opened her mouth to make a frantic denial of his suggestion, but she was too late.

Mrs Mayers had beaten her to it. 'Oh, yes, James.' She turned to Lark. 'That will be marvellous, Lark. James will be able to show you a little more of the city. I'm afraid I could be tied up for some time with the other committee members.'

Lark wanted to tell her that she would be quite happy having lunch on her own, but Mrs Mayers was already standing up, and so was James. Why on earth had James said he wanted to have lunch with her? It was the last thing she had expected.

Mrs Mayers had already left the breakfast-room, but James halted by the door. He was waiting for her, Lark recognised, her heart thumping nervously.

'Headache gone?'

Lark flushed uncomfortably. She had scribbled on her note that she wasn't feeling well and had a headache, a lie which James had plainly not believed.

'I don't want to have lunch with you,' she told him huskily.

'No...really?' She had forgotten his gift for sarcasm. 'Why not? Hoping to meet Hunter instead, were you?'

He sounded so savage. She started to tremble. 'James...'

'We need to talk,' he told her curtly, cutting right across her husky plea.

Despite having told herself that the last thing she wanted to do was to spend time with James, desperately trying to avoid having to endure the humiliation of listening to him telling her that last night was something they should both forget, Lark still couldn't resist the temptation to wear her new separates.

She told herself that it was because she didn't want to let Mrs Mayers down, but her heart knew differently. If she was going to have to endure James's rejection, then at least she would endure it with her head held high. What hurt most of all was that he actually thought he had to tell her that last night had been an aberration he never wanted to repeat. Did he honestly believe she was naïve enough to think that because he had made love to her it meant that he loved her? That she thought that a physical bond between two people was the equivalent of an emotional bond?

In the clear, bright sunlight of the New England morning, it was hard to believe that last night had ever taken place, and that it wasn't merely a fantasy conjured up by her imagination.

It would have been kinder of James to have simply left her with that delusion, she reflected sadly as she went back downstairs in good time to rejoin her employer.

She had changed, too, and she beamed approvingly at Lark's outfit. 'There, I told you they'd come in useful.'

James walked into the hall just in time to catch his mother's comment, his eyebrows lifting slightly. He looked paler than usual, Lark noticed, probably because he was suffering from jet lag.

And remorse?

Not remorse. More like resentment, she reflected, the cynicism of her thoughts reflected in her eyes. She avoided looking directly at him, even when he held open the door of the car for her.

There was plenty of room for all of them in the limousine, but still Lark was acutely conscious of him sitting beside her. She had elected to take the small seat behind the driver, thinking to leave a safe distance between them, but she had overlooked the length of James's legs, not anticipating that he would choose to sit directly opposite her and stretch them out either side of her, so that every time the car went round a bend its size and weight meant that there was a tendency for them to roll, which brought her into immediate physical contact with James.

'Lark, you look pale. Doesn't she, James?' Mrs Mayers said worriedly, breaking into her agonised thoughts. 'Are you finding the heat too much? It does sometimes take a while to adjust, and you have such delicate skin.'

Lark couldn't help it; a dark tide of colour washed right over her. Not just because of the way James was looking at her, but because she was remembering how this morning she had discovered small, dark bruises on her body; not uncomfortable in any way, but open reminders of the intensity with which she and James had made love.

Even now, with every logical reason there could be for her to regret what had happened, her body still thrilled to a quivering frisson of sensation at the memory.

'While you two are having lunch, I want to go and visit Jack,' Mrs Mayers commented, and Lark was grateful for the diversion her remark created, because she and James spent the next few minutes discussing her old friend and his health.

'Which reminds me,' she continued, 'Charlotte said you were both going down to visit her father at the weekend. How was he, James? Charlotte's father had a very bad fall some years ago, and is virtually housebound,' she explained to Lark. 'He refuses to use a wheelchair, and since he can only walk a very short distance... I don't see as much of him as I should. He's a charming man, Lark, an academic with a very dry sense

of humour. You'd never guess to speak to him that he
virtually ran off with Charlotte's mother. It was quite a
cause célèbre at the time. Her family were extremely
wealthy, and David, although he comes from a good
family, had nothing other than his salary. He was in the
navy in those days, and since Charlotte's mother was
under age—in those days one could not marry under the
age of twenty-one without one's parents' consent in
England—and so they ran away together.'

'To Gretna Green?' Lark asked, interested despite the
fact that it was Charlotte's parents they were discussing;
it was not their fault that she couldn't like their daughter,
she told herself reasonably.

'Oh, no, nothing so obvious. David's family owned
property in the Channel Islands, and he took her there.
By the time the families realised where they were, she
was hopelessly compromised, and of course her parents
had to give permission for them to marry. She told me
once that she and David were never actually lovers before
they married, but of course her parents didn't know that.'
She gave a small laugh. 'I suspect they expected Charlotte
to arrive far sooner than she actually did. I'm very fond
of David. How is he, James?'

'Much as always. The wet weather causes him a great
deal of discomfort; although of course he will never say
so. He's very concerned about the estate. He worries
about it being broken up once he's gone, but I assured
him that he had no cause to fear.'

'David inherited family property and land from a
cousin who died unexpectedly, which made him an extremely wealthy man. The estate has been in the family
since the time of Edward the Confessor. David would
very much like to see Charlotte married and with a
family.'

'He will do one day,' James assured his mother, and
Lark, remembering the way Charlotte had clung to his
arm and openly made it obvious how much she desired
him, wondered if this was the reason he wanted to speak

to her: to make it clear to her how very far apart their futures lay.

He had desired her, and in fulfilling that desire he had shown her great skill and tenderness, but when it came to commitment...to marriage... Her mouth went dry—the air-conditioning in the car, she told herself numbly.

In other circumstances, Lark would have found the committee meeting interesting. The subject under discussion was moral ethics involved in research on human embryos, and the standpoint the charity should take on such work.

By the time the meeting broke up they were no nearer a decision, committee members speaking with equal force and conviction on both sides.

'A complex issue,' Mrs Mayers said tiredly as she and Lark left. 'Of course, one wants to make progress, but ethically...' She shook her head. 'I really don't know.'

Lark didn't either, although she suspected that had she a child who desperately needed the knowledge such research could provide, she would be more than grateful for the results obtained by modern methods of research. It was a moral dilemma for which there was no easy answer.

James was waiting for them in the foyer of the building. He was glancing at his watch as they walked in, and frowning. No doubt wishing the interview with her over, Lark thought miserably.

What had happened to this morning's determination to remain cool and proud? Now she felt bowed down by the weight of her unhappiness.

Last night she had shared with this man the most intimate experience there was, giving the very essence of herself freely and joyously, without thought of what was to follow. Although she could never regret their love-making, what she did regret was her vulnerability to a man who was not worthy of having her love, a man who, moreover, had no trust in her honesty, no faith or belief in her; a man who had simply and briefly desired her body.

Even so, she could not simply sit there and let him reject her. Far better if she was the one to reject him, to let him know she had no more desire to prolong their intimacy than he had himself.

With this in mind, Lark made no protest when Mrs Mayers left her with James.

At first, when she recognised where their taxi was heading, she thought he must be taking her to the Bostonian, but once they had got out and he had paid off the driver she realised her error.

He saw her glancing at the imposing building, and smiled without humour before saying tightly, 'Given you a taste for the rich life, has he?'

When she refused to reply, he added savagely, 'Dear God, do you know what you're doing? Is that really what you want? A rich marriage with a man you can't desire?'

Lark's heart leapt jerkily in shock and anger. Who was he to accuse her? And where on earth had he got the idea that she was even contemplating marriage to Hunter? Heavens, she had only been out with the man twice! But, before she could say so, James took hold of her wrist, wrenching her round to face him, and making her wince with pain at the roughness of his movements.

'I can understand why he appeals to you, Lark, but if you were the least bit attracted to him, you would never have made love with me the way you did last night.'

She jerked away from him as though he had hurt her physically.

'You don't own me, James, just because we happened to make love last night.' Her head lifted, her chin tilting defiantly as she refused to let the tears she could feel pressing against her eyes betray her. 'In fact, as far as last night is concerned, it's something I just want to forget.'

There was a moment's tense silence, both of them oblivious to the curious and amused stares of passers-by who stopped to glance again at the handsome couple standing on the pavement, so involved in their own quarrel that they noticed no one else.

'Oh yes, I'm sure you do,' James snarled bitingly. 'But you won't. I'll guarantee that.'

Lark couldn't stand another moment of it. Not trusting herself to say another word without breaking down completely, she swung round on her heel and plunged into the mêlée of lunch-time strollers, desperate to escape.

She heard James call her name, but ignored him, hurrying desperately away from him, and not stopping until she realised that her side was aching with a stitch, and that she was in a completely unfamiliar area. In front of her was a huge, glassed-in building full of plants and flowers.

This was Fenueil Market, she realised, remembering what she had been told about the restored market area with its many boutiques and bars.

Dazed with shock and misery, she sank down on to a wooden bench, wondering that the sun should continue to shine and people continue to laugh when she was so desperately unhappy.

And what hurt most of all was that James should actually think that she was capable of encouraging Hunter for purely avaricious motives. That showed her more plainly than anything else the gulf between them. He was so blind to her real character, so bigoted and prejudiced, and yet despite that he had still made love to her.

How long she actually sat on the bench she didn't know, but at last she became conscious of the fact that the crowds were thinning out, that she was hungry and the sun was hot, that she was very tired and very alone.

She stood up shakily and then flinched as a hand touched her arm, but it wasn't James who stood watching her with concern, it was Hunter.

'Lark, my dear, are you all right? I saw you from across the road. What are you doing here on your own?'

'Oh, just passing the time exploring. I'm to rejoin Mrs Mayers at three,' she said.

'It's almost that now,' Hunter told her, glancing at his watch. 'Where are you meeting her? I'll drive you there. My car's only parked across the way. I had a business meeting in town.'

Lark was too exhausted to refuse, but her heart sank when Hunter stopped the car and she saw that Mrs Mayers and James were already at their arranged meeting-place—the Ritz foyer.

To judge from the genuinely warm way in which Mrs Mayers greeted them both, she had no idea what had happened between herself and James, Lark recognised thankfully.

And yet, as her employer commented on what a very small city Boston actually was, Lark was conscious of James's brooding, angry presence at her side. What right did he have to be angry? None! None at all. In fact, he should be feeling pleased and relieved, grateful that she was making it so easy for him to ignore last night.

They were all back in the limousine before he actually spoke to her, lifting her left hand as casually as though he had every right to do so, and studying her ring finger with grim intent before saying acidly, 'Not got it yet, I see. You'll have to try a little harder.'

'James!' Mrs Mayers exclaimed, frowning. 'What a very ungentlemanly thing to say! Hordes of young women may pursue *you*,' she added tartly, 'but I assure you that Lark is not of that genre.'

'No, she certainly isn't,' James agreed grimly, and Lark wondered if his mother was as aware as she was herself that the words were no compliment.

All in all, she reflected when she stepped out of the limousine at the Marble Head house, it had been a most disastrous day. All she wanted now was the privacy of her room, so that she could give way to the tears which had been threatening all day. But it was a release that she wasn't going to be granted.

Mrs Mayers wanted the notes of the meeting typed up, as she was having dinner with one of the doctors engaged on the research programme.

'Perhaps you'd join us as well, James,' she suggested to her son. 'I think we'd appreciate the legal view.'

'I'm no expert on medical ethics,' her son told her drily.

Lark flushed as she felt his hard gaze on her after she had muttered childishly under breath, 'Or any ethics at all.'

But it was only the truth, after all, she told herself rebelliously.

Mrs Mayers came into the study at six o'clock, just as Lark was finishing typing up the notes, to say that Hunter was on the phone.

'He wants to take you out to dinner.'

Lark pulled a face.

'I'm rather tired. I think I'll give it a miss.'

Hunter accepted her refusal good-naturedly. He was such a very kind man, Lark acknowledged as she replaced the receiver; it shouldn't be very difficult for a woman to fall in love with a man like him, especially a woman who needed tenderness and care in the way that she did. So why did she instead commit the ultimate folly of falling in love with James?

At least she was spared the ordeal of sitting opposite him at dinner. She ate with the Hennessys after James and his mother had left, and she suspected from the sympathetic glances Mary gave her from time to time that the other woman had guessed what was wrong, although she was far too tactful to say anything.

At nine o'clock, Lark went up to her room. There was only one course open to her now, dislike it though she did. She counted carefully through her money and then rang the airport. If she was prepared to fly stand-by, to arrive at the airport and wait for as long as it took to get a spare seat, she could just about manage the fare back across the Atlantic.

She knew that she ought to wait to speak personally with Mrs Mayers, but she also knew that if she delayed her resolve would weaken. The temptation to stay at least within contact of James was far too tempting, and that she should feel like that after all he had said showed her how very dangerous her position was. So she sat down to write a note to her employer, explaining as best she could why she was simply walking out and leaving her. And since this explanation could not be allowed in any way to refer to her feelings for Mrs Mayers' son, it proved an impossible task.

She had just crumpled up a fifth attempt and brushed away the defeated tears that kept on relentlessly destroying her concentration when a car drew up outside.

It was still far too early for Mrs Mayers and James to return, so it was probably someone visiting the Hennessys.

She thought no more about it, until she heard a firm rap on her door. Before she could respond, the door opened and James strode in.

'Lark, I...' he began in a peremptory tone, only to stop as he took in her tear-stained face and the discarded sheets of notepaper.

'What's going on?' he demanded frowningly, swooping on one of the crumpled sheets, before Lark could stop it.

She did try, though, reaching desperately for it, her voice husky and shocked as she begged, 'Please go away. I don't want to see you.'

'So it would seem,' James said slowly, having smoothed out and read her note. 'But why this... What is it? Are you frightened that I might tell Cabot that we've been lovers? Is that why you're running away?'

Lark's temper snapped. She stood up, her fingers clenching.

'I don't care what you tell Hunter. I don't care what you tell anyone. Do you think if I honestly wanted to have a relationship with him, I would even think of allowing another man to make love to me?'

Her eyes were brilliant with a rage that carried her beyond caution.

'You're the one who wants to pretend that last night never happened, James—not me. Did you really think I wouldn't realise that last night meant nothing to you, that it was just a momentary impulse? You don't know me at all. You've never known me. To you, I'm still the guilty party, the woman responsible for a major crime. You wanted to have lunch with me today, so that...'

'I wanted to have lunch with you today, so that I could tell you how wonderful you were last night,' he interrupted her softly. 'So that I could assure you that it wasn't just a one-night stand. Last night was your first time and...'

'And because you discovered that I was a virgin you want to behave like an old-fashioned hero and do the gentlemanly thing,' Lark flung at him acidly, so thoroughly confused by his words, and thrown with this abrupt volte-face, that it was hard to avoid betraying it. 'Well, there's no need. I'm a woman, not a child, and I'm perfectly capable of taking full responsibility for my own actions.'

This was worse, so much worse than she had expected. Didn't he realise that she loved him, and that to have him stand there in front of her and speak to her in the way he was was causing her the most unbearable pain?

She turned her head away from him, and then drew in her breath in a taut gasp as his fingers touched her skin, tracing the path of her recent tears, sending tiny pulses of sensation racing under her skin.

'And these?' he asked softly. When she refused to reply, he added more forcefully, 'And to set the record straight, I did not *discover* that you were a virgin,' he mimicked her words, making her skin burn. 'I was well aware of that fact before I touched you. For God's sake, Lark,' he exclaimed wryly, 'why the hell do you think I was so careful with you?'

That got her attention. She looked at him, her eyes rounding with the impact of his words, unable to conceal her shock.

'So innocent,' he said roughly, and suddenly it seemed to Lark that, although he hadn't moved, there was far less space between them; and the room was too hot, despite the whirr of the air-conditioning. She wanted to step back, but pride wouldn't let her.

'Did you really think I didn't know?' He seemed unable to believe it. 'Did you really think I wanted to forget what happened? Lark, why is it that you can't trust me? You drive me mad with jealousy by flaunting Cabot in my face. Didn't last night show you how I feel about you?'

'You still want me?'

She hadn't realised he had actually taken hold of her until she felt his arms tighten at her words, making her voice sound breathless and husky.

'Yes, I want you,' he told her fiercely. 'I want you, desire you, need you, ache for you...am almost obsessed by you to the point where all I want to do is to carry you off somewhere where I can be alone with you and make love with you.'

His voice had gradually grown more slurred, more heavy with sensual promise, and now her own senses, dazed by what he was saying, made her flesh respond to his nearness. She trembled slightly, already feeling the warmth of his breath on her skin, knowing that he was going to kiss her and feeling her body surge with anticipation of it, meeting his need with matching ardour. She could feel the heavy thud of his heart and the unmistakable arousal of his body as he groaned against her mouth and moved restlessly against her, trying to ease the fierce pulsing of his flesh.

His hands laced into her hair as he stilled her mouth beneath his own, kissing her with such savagery that she was forced to protest. He stopped immediately, cradling her head against his chest, frowning when he inspected the swollen fullness of her mouth.

'What are we doing to each other?' he groaned. 'I swear to God I've never hurt a woman like that before. Just tell me one thing, Lark—are you or do you intend to become involved with Cabot?'

Lark shook her head and told him honestly, 'I like Hunter, but that's all.'

'Then why the hell did you let me think——' James began impatiently, but Lark silenced him, placing her fingers against his lips.

'I thought you didn't want me. It was pride, James, although you were the one who suggested that Hunter and I were involved.'

She watched as he ran his fingers inside his loosened shirt collar. He looked hot and slightly dishevelled—a human being, vulnerable to all the human emotions and fears.

'You were going to leave,' he said flatly. 'If I hadn't come back you'd have been gone...'

'It seemed the only thing to do,' Lark told him.

There was a long pause, and then he looked at her and asked quietly, 'Because you hate me so much for last night?'

Lark shook her head, unable to look at him, her answer slow in coming, and very hesitant, as though she half regretted making the admission. 'I... I wanted you to make love to me. I don't regret that, I can't... But it hurt to believe that you knew so little about me that you thought I could make love with you and at the same time be contemplating a relationship with someone else. I hated knowing that you had made love with me, without having any respect for my judgement, without there being any trust...'

He was quiet for a long time, and then he took her hand and said wryly, 'Trust is a mutual thing, Lark. I could accuse you of having as little faith in me as you believe I have in you. Logically, perhaps, I shouldn't have been jealous of Cabot, but today I haven't been feeling particularly logical.'

It was an admission that startled her enough for her to tease, 'And you a practising barrister!'

She was stunned to see how angry he looked as he took hold of her and virtually shook her.

'Is that how you still see me? As the barrister? It was the *man* who made love to you last night, Lark. The man who went insanely jealous at the thought of you with someone else. The man who wants to take hold of you right now and lay you on that bed and...'

His voice had dropped, and its resonance sent a quiver right through her. She didn't need to close her eyes to conjure up images of the two of them entwined on her bed; she felt her legs weak with longing, her body arching toward him.

'Let's start again, Lark. Last night I rushed you. I should have taken time to...' He broke off and shook his head. 'You and I shared something very special last night, and I don't just mean the sex...'

'We can't be lovers, James,' Lark told him quickly. Her insides were already tied in knots of tension and pain. What was happening to her? She wanted this man and wanted him desperately, but how could she when he was her enemy? She feared him, she acknowledged painfully. She feared the powerful hold he already had on her emotions, and she feared her vulnerability to him. But most of all she feared the anomalies in her own nature that allowed her to desire a man for whom she should really only feel contempt and dislike.

It shocked her to hear him saying tersely, 'We already are—remember? And I'm not talking about us simply being lovers, Lark. I'm talking about us having a relationship, about...'

'No!'

He stared at her, as the sharp, high sound of her denial fell away.

'Why not?' he asked, his quiet voice in direct contrast to her own panic. 'Because you work for my mother? Because of the court case?'

Lark looked at him, hoping he wouldn't see the pain in her eyes.

'Yes,' she told him huskily. 'There has to be trust between two people, James. You don't trust me, and I don't...I don't trust you,' she added, not seeing the anguish that flared briefly in his eyes as she looked away.

The silence seemed to stretch for a long time, and then he said, 'Trust isn't something that grows overnight. It's a slow plant and has to be nurtured. Granted, the circumstances in which we met weren't exactly ideal...'

There was no missing the irony in his voice, but Lark refused to respond to it.

'Give me two months, Lark. If at the end of that time...'

His plea startled her.

'James, it's no use,' she protested thickly. 'Why are you doing this?'

'Because I'm in love with you, you little fool,' he told her roughly. 'And what's more, I think you love me too, only you're too stubborn to admit it.'

She couldn't say a word. She could only stare at him while his words sank slowly into her numb brain. He was in love with her... Impossible... Impossible... But what if it wasn't? What if he was telling the truth? What if, like her, he was powerless to resist the magnetic lure she had experienced that first day in court? What if...

'Two months, Lark,' he persisted huskily. 'Give me two months to prove to you that we can build something together...That you can trust me.'

Somehow or other she was in his arms, her answer in the kiss they exchanged. She could feel the dampness on his skin and marvelled at her ability to create such an emotional trauma within him.

Could it be true? Had he fallen in love with her? Some part of her mind still held on to its fears and doubts, reluctant to let them go, reluctant to believe, but Lark ignored it. She wanted to believe him, wanted to acknowledge that different, compassionate side of his nature and forget the way he had looked at her in court, the way he had refused to believe her. And yet...

'James, if the case hadn't been dismissed...if your mother hadn't offered me this job...I'm so grateful to her, you know...'

All her doubts showed in her voice. He looked at her, and she had the impression that he wanted to say something. He looked both tired and sad, and she wanted to reach out and stroke the lines of care from his face.

'All right, we won't talk about it,' she said softly, and yet, even as they kissed, she was wondering how on earth they could build a relationship on such a flimsy foundation. The past wouldn't go away simply because James didn't want to discuss it. Perhaps she should make him talk to her about it, but before she could say anything they heard a car outside.

'That will be Mother.'

'The dinner party...' Lark stared at him.

'I'd better go to my room. She'll be wanting to find out if my headache has gone. I had to come back and see you, and so I used the most basic excuse I could find.'

Instead of simply telling his mother the truth, Lark brooded, but it was difficult to hold on to the thought when James was kissing her, his hands whispering silken promises against her skin of pleasure to come.

They broke apart reluctantly.

'Tomorrow we'll have the whole day to ourselves...'

'I'm here to work, James,' Lark reminded him gently. 'I can't just desert your mother.'

'I'll fix it. I'll tell her that I need to talk to you about the ball at my place,' he teased her, but after he had gone Lark hoped that he wouldn't persuade Mrs Mayers to give her extra time off by deceiving her. She didn't like lying, but until the trial period they'd agreed on was up, she didn't want to involve anyone else. It was just one more thing that made the whole relationship difficult...

CHAPTER EIGHT

THEY had almost a week together and, far from having to ask Mrs Mayers for time off, that lady announced that since this was Lark's first visit to New England, and since she herself had more invitations than she could possibly fulfil from old friends, none of whom would be of the slightest interest to her son or her assistant, James should show Lark something of New England.

'Of course, it is at its most beautiful in the fall, and Cape Cod has become terribly touristy now, but there are still some lovely spots. I remember when I was a girl...the whole family would move out to the Cape for the summer.' She gave a reminiscent smile. 'Only my father stayed in the city.'

Lark tried to protest that she was in New England to work, but Mrs Mayers overruled her.

'Lark, if you are to work, then so must I. We've achieved so much already that I feel I owe it to myself to take some time off. If you refuse, you'll make me feel guilty. After all, you haven't had a full day off since you came to work for me.'

It was true, although Lark could have protested that her day's work was hardly as arduous as working a normal office routine would have been.

Later, looking back, the short space of time they had together seemed iridescent, like a soap bubble. And, like a soap bubble, fragile too.

They laughed, they talked, but never about the court case or events leading up to it. Was that because both of them were wary of treading on ground which they knew to be unsafe? Lark put the thought behind her. It was pointless to destroy the present because of the past,

144

but the past was what shaped the present and the future, she reflected uneasily.

James had driven them out to a remote part of the coast on their last day. There was no beach here, no sand, just huge slabs of rock carved by the tide. Around the corner of the headland was a small fishing village. Once, its deep-water harbour had been home for a small whaling fleet, and they had visited the local museum with its artefacts from those times. James had bought her a small piece of scrimshaw carved by a long-ago sailor. Slightly yellow with age, it had obviously been a love token from his sweetheart, the letter 'L' carved with small flowers and leaves. What had her name been? Louise? Lucy? Laura? She would never know, Lark reflected as she touched it. She was wearing it on a fine gold chain that James had also bought for her.

'Tonight I'm going to take you for a clam chowder supper,' James told her lazily, raising his prone body slightly so that he could look at her. 'You can't visit New England without trying Boston's speciality.'

Lark had already heard about the famous dish from Mrs Mayers, but she teased James by announcing that she never ate fish.

They had been sunbathing, taking advantage of the afternoon heat. James was already well tanned; her skin, paler and more delicate, needed protecting, and she had moved out of the sun into the shade several minutes before, to sit crouched on a boulder, with her arms round her knees. James was lying a couple of yards in front of her, the frayed denim shorts he had worn for swimming clinging damply to his skin. She wondered if he was wearing them for her benefit, or simply because the beach was not private enough for him to risk taking them off. Remembering the all-over golden hue of his body, she knew that he must have sunbathed in the nude before.

They hadn't made love a second time—at least, not properly; and there were times when she almost wished that James would not kiss or touch her when to do so meant that he left her raw and aching inside. She wished she had both the experience and the self-confidence to ask him to fulfil her, and wondered at the same time how it was that he somehow or other managed to control his own desire. Surely it was the male of the species who went out of control with physical desire, not the female?

'I have to leave in the morning,' James told her abruptly.

She had known it must happen; he had said all along that he could not stay more than a few days. He had even discussed with her the case he would shortly be taking to court. His very obvious involvement with his work, the depth of attention and concentration he gave it, had left her feeling a little shut out at times, and she also found it hard to equate the very obviously caring and concerned attitude he took to his clients with the callous way he had treated her, but it was a subject she preferred not to discuss. What would be the point? Besides, to do so raised other spectres. She hadn't spoken to him about it, but surely the mere fact that he never mentioned the case proved that he still did not believe she had been innocent?

That he was prepared to overlook her guilt surely must say something about the depths of his feelings for her. So why was she haunted by doubts about their relationship?

'At least we shan't be apart for too long. Mother intends to fly home in a couple of weeks, and I've persuaded her that both of you must come down to Abbotsfield. I want you to see it.'

Her heart soared. He wanted her to see his home.

'You love it, don't you?' she guessed, reading behind the almost curt words.

'Yes... Heredity is a very strange thing. I never gave the place a thought while I was growing up. But now I look at it and see, not just the bricks and mortar, but all those people who have gone before me... who've cherished and protected it...' He broke off with a grimace. 'Now you're letting me get maudlin. How many tickets is Mother expecting to sell? I'm hoping we can keep people out of the house itself.

'I'm going to miss you,' he added softly, watching the shadows play across her face. There was still so much of herself she kept hidden from him, still so much reserve she wouldn't allow him to penetrate. And he dared not rush her.

'I'll probably be too busy to notice you've gone,' Lark lied.

Just looking at him made her body ache, and she knew that her skin was flushed. She could feel her nipples harden and felt a wave of shame scorch her. Once... He had made love to her just once, and ever since then she had ached for him to do it again. But he hadn't... Why?

'Time we were going, I think. I'd like us to have dinner with Mother tonight, as it's my last evening. Do you mind? We can go out later on for that clam chowder.'

Of course she didn't mind; she already felt guilty at the amount of time they had spent together, but Mrs Mayers had refused to allow her to work. It was true that she had a very wide circle of friends, all of whom wanted to spend time with her.

Hunter had rung on several occasions to ask her out, and Lark had felt guilty about refusing him. She found it hard to believe that James had been jealous of him. There was just no comparison between them, or the way she felt about them.

Although Mary had outdone herself to provide them with an excellent meal, Lark felt that the occasion was overshadowed with an almost tangible aura of melancholy. Or was it just because she was already dreading parting from James?

Instead of bringing her self-confidence and security, their relationship had only heightened her awareness of how emotionally dependent she had become. She still felt as though their relationship was a very unequal one.

She had been quiet all through dinner, and now, on the way into Boston, she was conscious of James watching her, whenever his concentration on his driving allowed.

'You're very quiet,' he commented. 'Is something wrong?'

She knew that her smile was stiff, but it was the best she could do.

'Not really. I think these last few days have made me lazy. Holidays are like that, aren't they?'

She had deliberately avoided saying anything more personal. He must know how much she was going to miss him, how much she was dreading tomorrow.

He didn't say anything for a while, and she thought he was not going to bother to make any comment, until he suddenly swung the car into a parking spot and switched off the engine.

'Is that how you see our relationship, Lark? A holiday from reality... something that isn't really part of the fabric of your life?'

He was questioning her much as he had done in court, throwing the words at her in a hard, unfamiliar voice.

She wetted her lips with her tongue, her throat dry and taut. 'James, I... We've known each other for such a short space of time...'

'Long enough for us to become lovers.'

Yes, and that was part of the problem. Whenever she had visualised having a relationship with a man, she had expected that they would grow gradually towards sexual intimacy, never dreaming she would experience its explosive demanding force so intensely or so quickly.

'Are you trying to tell me that you're having second thoughts?'

Lark couldn't say anything, frightened by what her insecurities had led her to. Was this James's subtle way of breaking off from her? If so, it was a game she couldn't play.

'Are you?' she countered huskily, and heard him make an explosive sound in his throat.

'No, damn you, I'm not!' he told her thickly, reaching for her and dragging her into his arms. 'Oh, God, it was a crazy idea to do this tonight.' His fingers were shaping her face, touching her skin as though he couldn't get enough of the feel of it. 'Do you know what I want to do right now? I want to take you to bed and make love to you.'

She started to tremble. She couldn't help it, and he felt the reaction of her body and his own surged strongly against her.

She heard James curse, and then he was kissing her as though he was starving for the taste of her, and she was kissing him back, not caring that only the darkness outside the car prevented passers-by from seeing them.

She felt a rush of cool air against her skin and realised that he had unfastened the buttons of her shirt. His hands cupped her breasts and she moaned against his mouth, instinctively pressing herself as close to him as she could.

That she would actually have let him make love to her there in the car was something she couldn't deny, she reflected shakily later, when the sound of a car backfiring some way down the block had brought home to them both exactly where they were.

James had released her, pushing his hand through his hair, as though he was as confused and disturbed as she was herself by the intensity of their physical communication.

As he moved to switch on the engine, she saw quite clearly in the light from the street the arousal of his body.

'Don't,' he told her in a strained voice. 'Don't look at me like that, or I swear to God, I'll stop this damn car right here and make love to you in the street.'

After that, neither of them spoke. James drove back to Marble Head at a speed Lark was sure was in excess of the limit, but she said nothing. Her body was aching just as much as his, every tiny pulse reminding her that it was a week since they had made love.

There was a note for them in the hall.

'Decided to have an early night and take a sleeping pill,' Mrs Mayers had written, 'so that I can be up in time to see James in the morning before he leaves.'

Was Mrs Mayers being extraordinarily tactful, or had fate simply decided to be kind?

Without a word, they walked upstairs. When they reached her bedroom door, James paused very deliberately. He was giving her the opportunity to change her mind, Lark realised, and her heart soared. She must mean something to him, after all. She wasn't just someone for whom he felt physical desire.

'Did you really know that I was a virgin?' she asked him when they were undressed and lying on her bed, bathed by the moon shadows from the window.

'Yes,' he told her rawly.

A faint shadow touched her face, and she shivered slightly. He was such an experienced man. Had she disappointed him with her lack of skill?

'I'd been thinking about you while I swam.' The words were low, and she had to strain to catch them. 'And then, suddenly, there you were. You looked at me, and you went on looking, and I knew that there was no way I was going to be able to stop myself from touching you.'

He touched her now, stroking her hair and then caressing the smooth curves of her body.

'On the beach I made love to *you*, Lark.' His mouth touched her skin, drawing bursts of fire from her nerve-endings as its moist warmth trailed down over her jaw to her throat. 'One day soon I'm going to teach you how to make love to me.'

She swallowed hard and then demanded breathlessly, 'Show me now, James.'

How elastic time could be, stretching to unimaginable lengths and then concertinaing into little more than the blink of an eye. In retrospect, that was how that night seemed to Lark: short, fevered bursts of passion when she cried out beneath the skill of James's hands and mouth; seconds which seemed to encapsulate whole lifetimes when their mutual desire caused the firmament to explode around them while they floated free; oases of peace while they slept, only to wake and touch again; and then a time when James left her just before dawn which seemed to stretch into eternity as the last minutes before his departure taunted her with what she was going to have to endure once he was gone.

He left immediately after breakfast, refusing to allow them to accompany him to the airport. Lark stayed in the background. Her eyes were heavy with passion and lack of sleep, and she didn't want to draw attention to her appearance.

And then, abruptly, he was gone.

'How empty the house seems without a man in it,' Mrs Mayers commented wistfully when the car had left. 'James is far too old to live at home, of course, and I hope I'm not a clinging mother, but at times like this I do miss him quite dreadfully. Are you all right, Lark?' she asked kindly. 'You look pale.'

Lark froze, unable to say a word until Mrs Mayers, oblivious to her shock, added, 'Did you enjoy our famous Boston clam chowder?'

Lark hated to lie. She swallowed hard and then said huskily, 'Actually, I never had any. Neither of us were hungry when we got to Boston, so we came back.'

She went flame-red as Mrs Mayers turned to look at her. After giving her a shrewd look, her employer said calmly, 'Well, Mary did rather excel herself with dinner, and I'm sure there'll be another opportunity to taste it before we leave.'

Two weeks later, as their plane circled above Heathrow, Lark reflected that she had still not tasted the famous Boston dish, but she didn't really mind.

Two brief and unsatisfactory telephone calls from James had left her aching to see him, and in his absence all her doubts had come crowding back into her mind. It had never been Lark's habit to discuss her private feelings with other people, but now she longed to have someone with whom she could share her insecurities.

It was early evening before they arrived back at the St John's Wood house, and, despite the mountain of post in the study, Mrs Mayers insisted that neither of them were going to touch it until the morning.

Three extremely busy days followed when she didn't see or hear from James at all. She knew that he was involved in an extremely complicated court case being tried out of London, but even so, every time the telephone rang, she found herself tensing in anticipation of hearing his voice.

Would it have made it better or worse if her employer had known of their relationship?

Right from the start, Lark had been opposed to Mrs Mayers' knowing about their involvement, and yet, when James had asked her why, she hadn't been able to give him an answer.

Perhaps it had something to do with the way she had been brought up, and the very physical nature of the bond she shared with James.

Or was she perhaps worried that, if Mrs Mayers knew about their relationship, she might feel obliged to dismiss her should it end? Lark didn't know, and, although James had not been able to understand her feelings, he had given way to them in the end.

By the end of the week she was exhausted—the combination of her sleepless nights aching for James, and the sheer volume of work she was getting through during the day, draining her of every last bit of energy. On Friday evening, all she wanted to do was to go to bed and sleep.

Mrs Mayers had gone out for dinner, her final words to Lark being an instruction that she was not to carry on working.

That had been at six o'clock. At eight, Lark took the final letter out of her typewriter and switched it off. In their absence the new computer equipment had been installed, but it was having a few teething problems which meant that it wasn't working at full efficiency as yet, and Lark had not had any time to spare to play around with it. That would have to wait until the backlog of work was cleared.

The meal that Cora had brought through on a tray was still untouched on her desk, and she grimaced faintly at the congealing contents of the plates.

It was Cora's evening off, but, even though Lark hadn't eaten anything since her early lunch, she felt too exhausted to go into the kitchen and raid the fridge.

What she intended to do was to go and have a long soak in the bath and then go straight to bed. It had even crossed her mind to ask Mrs Mayers for one of her sleeping tablets, but she had resisted the impulse.

She had just switched off the lights in the study when she heard a key in the front door.

Perhaps because she was so tired, it never even occurred to her that it might be James, and so she was totally unprepared for the sight of him in the doorway, tall and imposing in a formal dark suit, his face tired beneath its tan.

The shock of seeing him held her motionless, simply watching as he dropped the briefcase he was carrying, and kicked the door closed behind him, at the same time reaching with his free hand to tug off his tie and unfasten the top buttons of his shirt.

It had been a hot day, with the threat of thunder making the air oppressive and tainted with the smell of sulphur. Lark could smell the heat on James's body as he came towards her, shedding his jacket which he threw casually on to a chair.

Her heart started to beat far too fast, her voice slightly breathless as she exclaimed, 'James!'

'Oh, God, I've missed you!'

She was in his arms without really knowing how she had got there, thrilling to the muted savagery of his kiss as his mouth closed over her own with hungry dominance.

She felt the thrust of his tongue and teased it daringly until James pushed her back against the wall, leaning into her so that she could feel the pulsing hardness of his body, his fingers tangling in her hair, holding her head so that she couldn't move while he proceeded to demonstrate how dangerous her teasing had been. The grinding movement of his body against her own was evidence of his frustration. His hands gripped her thighs. Her body went weak, melting with pleasure.

She heard him groan as he fitted himself against her, and she gasped with shock as she felt his hands on her skirt, trying to manoeuvre it out of the way.

'James! No, not here...' she protested, but her body did not share her shock, wantonly welcoming his urgency. Her breasts pushed eagerly against the fabric of her shirt, her nipples plainly outlined, tight and hard. The sight of her arousal momentarily distracted him, and he released her skirt and, instead, unfastened her shirt, his fingers clumsy and urgent, so that he tore one of the buttonholes in his eagerness to touch her.

What had happened to the finesse of his earlier love-making? Lark wondered dazedly, as he tugged at the confining fabric of her bra to expose the soft globe of her breast.

She heard him mutter something she couldn't catch, and then the breath left her lungs in a gasp of shock and pleasure as he took her nipple into his mouth, raking the tender flesh with his teeth, over and over again, until she was crying out in arousal and moving her hips against him with quick, jerky movements, caught up in a thundering race of desire that obliterated everything else.

She had forgotten where they were, racked by the need to feel his flesh plunging within her own, filling her, pleasuring her, and finally easing the ache that had suddenly become the focus of her world.

Somehow James's shirt had become undone, although she had no remembrance of doing so. The soft, dark hair on his chest was soaked with sweat. She could feel it dampening her palms as she pressed them against him while she returned his kiss, this time responding feverishly to the ever-increasing thrust of his tongue.

She felt his hands on her clothes and pressed eagerly against him, sliding her arms around his back so that she could rub her breasts against his chest, her body writhing as though it were beyond her control when she was finally free of the constriction of her underwear.

She heard the rasp of his zipper as he lifted her off the floor, and she instinctively wrapped herself around him, welcoming each shuddering thrust of his body, feeling him fill her and surround her with his maleness.

Outside, thunder crashed and rolled, but neither of them heard it, oblivious to everything but the storm they themselves were creating.

Sensations exploded inside her, not in ripples, but in huge, crashing waves that made her bite frantically into James's skin, her nails digging sharp crescents into his body as they shared the feverish culmination of their lovemaking.

Her body was reluctant to let him go; a tiny echo of sensation, a sensual promise of pleasure still to be, made her cling to him, holding him within her with a wantonness she had never dreamed she would ever know.

'Again.'

She heard herself say the word, and was shocked as much by the drunken, satiated satisfaction in her voice as by what she had actually said.

Her eyes opened wide, shocked and confused, her gaze trapped in the glittering, metallic brilliance of the look James returned.

What she had said had excited him, possessed him almost, and she protested when she felt him move inside her, shocked both by what she had said and how she had felt.

'James. No...'

It wasn't really her, that wild, wanton creature who had cried out for him to kindle that taunting flicker of sensation until it became full-blown need, who had been aching to experience, over and over again, the thrill of knowing that the sensation of moving within her brought him to mindless subjugation to his need.

But he wasn't listening to her protest; his gaze was fixed steadily on her as he moved slowly and deliberately.

A tiny thrill of fear-edged pleasure fluttered through her. She was unable to drag her gaze from his, unable to stop herself from responding to what he was doing, and yet conscious of a moment's stark recognition of the complexity of emotions, for she had just done something she would once have sworn she could never do.

She had just said 'no' when they both knew she meant 'yes', but even as she tried to come to terms with the anomaly she saw James's eyes darken and glaze, and knew that he was slipping just as out of control as she was herself—both of them slaves of a need enforced by nature itself.

This time the climax was long and slow, leaving her so drained that she was completely unable to move, and it was James who picked up their discarded clothing and guided her upstairs to her room.

'I can't stay much longer,' he told her quietly. 'In fact, I shouldn't be here at all. I hope to God the jury is still out, otherwise I'm going to end up being disbarred.'

Lark couldn't believe what she was hearing; he had actually driven all the way from the trial to be with her, risking his career and reputation simply because his need for her drove him so intensely.

It reassured her and yet disturbed her at the same time.

Despite the time they had spent together, it seemed almost as though they had no point of contact other than as lovers.

James was far too intelligent a man not to want much more from the woman to whom he gave his love, and that made Lark shiver a little, conscious of how little she actually knew about James's hopes and ambitions. Had she been wrong to believe him when he said that he loved her, that he wanted their relationship to grow? Was it only as a bedmate that he really saw her? Had she been deceiving herself in thinking that he would come to return her love?

It all went back to one thing: a lack of trust. For differing reasons, neither of them trusted the other. If they did, she would have been able to ask him freely and openly how he envisaged their future; as it was...

As it was, she had to hide her insecurities from him, and watch as he walked away from her, promising that he would get in touch with her as soon as he could.

CHAPTER NINE

SHE loved him. Lark had no doubts at all about that. What she did have doubts about, though, were the very basic inequalities in their relationship. Those inequalities gave rise to doubts, all the more painful because of her inability to express them. Her instincts and her upbringing shrieked to her that two people who did not share mutual trust and respect could never have a successful relationship, and James did not respect or trust her. He couldn't do.

Despite the backlog of work, which proved to be even more heavy than Mrs Mayers had forecast, Lark still had time to brood on her personal doubts. If James was really serious about allowing their relationship to develop, surely he would have wanted to discuss with her the court case, to hear her side of the story, to have her exonerate herself? Yet the subject was never mentioned. But that didn't mean that it wasn't there. Perhaps he was waiting for her to raise the subject, but Lark was reluctant to do so.

He had already disbelieved her once, publicly, in court, and when she was honest with herself she was forced to admit that, if he refused to believe her, she wasn't quite sure what she should do. Pride would demand that she should terminate their relationship, but did she have the strength of will to do that?

She knew that it was possible to love someone without respecting them, but did she honestly want that type of love, or was she just being unrealistic? Perhaps James was quite content not to know the truth. After all, one didn't necessarily have to like or respect a person with whom one had a brief affair.

Was that all she was to him? A brief affair? He hadn't led her to think so, but then, she acknowledged cynically, few men would. Yet, as she had come to know James better, she had judged him to be a man scrupulously honest in his dealings with others, no matter how painful that honesty might be to himself or to them.

It was six days before she saw him again, and six days was a long time in which powerful doubts could fester. They nagged at her at her most vulnerable moments, mute but goading voices that wouldn't be denied.

Mrs Mayers remarked with concern that she was looking tired, and asked if she was working her too hard. Lark denied it instantly.

She was well organised with the preliminary arrangements for the ball. A date had been arranged at Mrs Mayers' suggestion for herself and Lark and the company who were to provide the marquee to visit James's house to check on the suitability of the site. Mrs Mayers had not said if James would be there, and Lark hadn't liked to ask.

He telephoned her unexpectedly one afternoon, her heart racing at the sound of his voice. He told her that the case was over, and then went on to add that he wouldn't be able to see her that evening.

Perhaps her silence conveyed her feelings to him, because he suddenly added thickly, 'I'm coming round now, Lark.'

'Your mother will be pleased to see you,' she told him weakly, still trying to come to terms with the jolt of emotions she had felt at the sound of his voice. 'She needs to talk to you about some of the arrangements for the ball.'

After she had replaced the receiver, she went in search of Mrs Mayers.

'James has just been on the phone,' she told her, conscious of a slight flush staining her face. 'He's coming round.'

'To see me?' Mrs Mayers enquired, her eyebrows lifting slightly, and Lark felt her flush deepen.

'I . . . I told him you'd probably want to discuss the arrangements for the ball with him.' She knew that she sounded flustered, and felt even more so when Mrs Mayers laughed.

'Did you? Well, I'm sure that's not what's bringing him hot-footing round here, Lark. Please don't be embarrassed,' she added in a gentle tone. 'I have no wish to interfere between you, but it was rather obvious to me in Boston that my son was very smitten. He doesn't make a habit of flying over to see me at a moment's notice,' she added in a rather dry voice.

'I . . . I hope you don't mind,' Lark said awkwardly, but her hesitant words were brushed aside.

Mrs Mayers' eyebrows rose sharply and she exclaimed very forthrightly, 'Good heavens, Lark, of course I don't mind! Why on earth should I? If James chooses to ask you out and you choose to accept, that is entirely your own affair, my dear. What on earth made you think I would mind?' she questioned.

The court case, her own position in Mrs Mayers' household, her family's lack of status and wealth, all flashed through Lark's mind, but she couldn't say anything. As though Mrs Mayers had read her mind, her employer said in a very kind voice, 'Lark, my dear, I like you. I liked you from the very first moment we met, and that liking has increased during the time you've worked for me. I've been telling James for a long while that it's high time he found himself a wife and provided me with some grandchildren.' She eyed Lark with a teasing smile, and then added in a more serious tone, 'I'm glad that the two of you have been able to sort out your differences, Lark, and if my son does manage to persuade you to become a member of this family, I shall be delighted to welcome you to it.' She gave Lark a kiss, smiling at her confusion and then said teasingly, 'As far as the arrangements for the ball are concerned, I think

I can probably leave it to you to discuss them with James, don't you?'

Did Mrs Mayers really see her as a prospective daughter-in-law, or was she just being kind? Lark wondered as she walked back to the study. Had she perhaps realised how very deeply in love with James she was? But she had been wrong about one thing—she and James had not sorted out their differences.

She was still frowning when he walked into the office ten minutes later. He was dressed formally in a business suit of fine dark wool, cufflinks glinting in the crisp, white, starched cuffs of his shirtsleeves. Who was it who ironed them to such perfection? Lark wondered bemusedly, suddenly acutely self-conscious and shy.

Had she and this man really shared the most intimate physical act that there was? He reached out and traced the faint frown lines on her forehead, and at his touch her shyness disappeared.

'Why the frown?' he asked huskily.

'No reason. I was just wondering who ironed your shirts?'

'I have two live-in Filipino maids,' he told her coolly. 'Twin sisters of nineteen. They were working in a hotel I visited during a conference, and they were desperate to get work over here, so I brought them back with me. They're extremely obliging.'

He said it in such a way, with such a look on his face, that Lark was instantly outraged, her eyes flashing dark with resentment both at his patronising tone towards her sex and at the thought of him sharing his home with two young and no doubt extremely lovely young women.

When he saw her expression he laughed, and Lark could almost have hit him.

'Idiot,' he told her softly, sliding his hand into her hair and tugging it gently. 'I have them laundered at an establishment run by an extremely plump and middle-aged Chinese couple and their son.'

'You deliberately tried to make me jealous!' Lark stormed at him.

'And succeeded,' he agreed lazily. He was still holding her hair, and refused to let it go, even though she tried to pull away.

'I don't consider it was very funny.' She was still too wrought up by the shock of her jealousy to react rationally. She actually felt almost shaky with relief that he had been teasing her, and yet resentful at the same time that he had taken advantage of her feelings for him.

'I'm sorry.' His instant apology and the serious note of concern in his voice disarmed her. 'Call it a small recompense for the agony you put me through with Hunter Cabot.'

His reminder that he, too, had experienced jealousy was all that was needed to banish the last remnants of her anger. She was still in his arms ten minutes later, when the study door was opened peremptorily and Charlotte stalked in.

Immediately James released her, leaving Lark feeling vulnerable and at a disadvantage in front of the other girl. Today Charlotte was wearing expensive Italian casuals, a huge pink suede blouson jacket worn over an extremely short and tight-fitting black skirt and matching top. She shook her head slightly as she walked, so that her hair rippled sleekly.

Totally ignoring Lark, she said to James, 'Ah, there you are, darling. I wanted to talk to you about this do we're going to tonight. Your chambers said you were here.'

She linked her arm through James's as she spoke, drawing him back towards the open door. 'Do excuse us, won't you?' she threw over her shoulder in a sugar-sweet tone to Lark as they disappeared. 'I expect that you have absolutely tons of work to do.'

'Why didn't you let me know you were back in town, darling?' Lark heard her saying to James as they walked away. 'I've missed our regular lunch dates.'

She ought to have realised that James was just teasing her about his Filipino housemaids, Lark reflected bitterly as she got up and slammed the door behind them with unnecessary violence. Why would he need them when he had Charlotte, ready and all too willing to provide whatever kind of services he wanted?

'Bitch,' she chided herself as she settled herself back behind her typewriter. There was a kind of family connection between James and Charlotte, that was all. It was hardly his fault if the woman deliberately teased and flirted with him every time she saw him.

But still Lark felt hurt that James had not made it more obvious to Charlotte that he did not appreciate her attentions. Any woman listening to that brief and very deliberate conversation would have been left in no doubt at all that the relationship between them was more than simply friends, and Lark was well aware Charlotte had wanted her to believe that she and James had been lovers. But was it true? Even if it was, was it any concern of hers? Lark questioned herself. It was unrealistic to expect that there had been no other women in his life, but did one of them have to have been Charlotte? she reflected savagely as she ripped the sheet of paper out of the machine and screwed it up.

What was really bugging her was Charlotte's arch comment about their date tonight. When James had told her that he wouldn't be able to see her in the evening, she had assumed that it was because of a business meeting of some kind, not a date with another woman.

It was nearly three-quarters of an hour before he returned, and by that time Lark had worked herself up into a state of furious resentment. She kept on typing when he walked into the study, stopping only to give him a cool smile as she shuffled some papers beside her machine.

'Sorry about that,' he apologised easily, 'but Charlotte wanted to discuss a few things with me.'

Lark only just managed to bite back a cynical, 'Yes, and I can imagine what they were.' Instead, she offered a smile which merely stretched her lips and did nothing to warm the coldness of her eyes.

'Now...' James said softly, perching beside her on the edge of her desk, one hand on her machine, the other reaching out deftly to twist an errant curl of hair round his forefinger.

Lark did not deign to react by tugging her head out of the way, as she felt inclined. It smacked too much of childish tantrums to behave like that, much as she longed to do so.

As he leaned forward she saw the fabric of his trousers pull against the solid muscles of his thighs, and against her will her senses stirred. Her unwanted reaction to him only made her the more determined to resist his attempt to take her back in his arms.

'If you've got time, I need to discuss one or two points about the ball,' she said swiftly, avoiding looking directly at him. She didn't think she had the strength of mind to do that, not when she suspected that the look in his eyes was the same caressing and intimate one he had given her when he had first walked into the room. Then it had sent her pulse-rate rocketing out of control.

Now, now there was nothing she wanted more than the reassurance of his arms around her, but she was stubbornly determined to cling on to her pride. Why should she pretend that she didn't mind that he was taking Charlotte out for the evening?

'What's wrong?' he said quietly. 'Is it because I'm taking Charlotte out this evening? If so...'

She immediately tensed and interrupted, 'There's nothing wrong. I'm just rather tired. I've been out myself for the last couple of evenings,' she added, marvelling at her own ability to lie, 'and I'm rather looking forward to an early night.'

'I see.' James released her abruptly, suddenly coolly distant.

'I've got all the schedules for the ball,' Lark told him briskly, deliberately ignoring the pain tightening like a band round her heart.

'I'm afraid I don't have time to see them now.' James was equally brisk. 'If you give my secretary a ring and discuss it with her...'

'Your mother's arranged for us to go down to your home on the eighteenth,' Lark told him, her emotions betrayed by the sudden hectic spots of colour that appeared in her cheeks. 'The caterers and the people who provide the marquee are going to be there.'

'I'm not sure if I shall be free.'

This was the man she remembered from the court: arrogant, distant, totally different from the man who had held her in his arms such a very short time ago.

She let him go with her misery forming a tight, hard ball in her throat, determined not to call him back or to say one word that would acknowledge her pain.

He opened the door and hesitated briefly, but Lark had already bent her head over her typewriter. She could almost feel his anger. It filled the room, encompassing her in its heat, and yet for all that, when he left the room, he closed the door behind him as quietly and gently as though he had been afraid of waking a sleeping child.

And that was another thing—she had been going to tell him that they had been lucky, and that that first passionate but unprotected consummation between them had not resulted in a child. Hurt, and angry as much with herself as she was with him, Lark refused to leave the study until Mrs Mayers came in search of her, expressing concern when she discovered that she was still working.

'Is James taking you out tonight?' she asked.

Lark shook her head, unable to trust her ability to conceal her feelings from her employer. 'He already had a commitment,' she said when she could, adding bitterly, 'with Charlotte.'

If Mrs Mayers was aware of the depth of her feelings, she didn't let it show. Instead she said lightly, 'Charlotte is extremely attached to him. I think she sees him as a substitute older brother.' She smiled. 'There was a time, shortly after she was born, when her mother and I planned for the two of them to be married,' she chuckled, but Lark couldn't share her amusement.

The cold fingers of doubt were growing, spreading long, icy tentacles that now reached out to taint every part of her relationship with James. What did she really mean to him—a momentary diversion?

Even though she wasn't tired, Lark went to bed early, as she had told James she intended to. She didn't sleep though, tormenting herself with mental images of him with Charlotte.

When she woke up, it was with half-remembered dreams about Charlotte, laughing at her, taunting her that James didn't really care.

As though her dreams were in some way an omen, Charlotte arrived just after lunch, when Mrs Mayers was having her daily rest.

She walked into the study unannounced, wearing a clinging polka-dotted yellow silk dress that fitted every voluptuous curve. Lark felt dowdy in comparison, and for the first time in her life actively envied another woman's wardrobe.

'James isn't here,' Lark told her shortly, in no mood to pander to the other girl.

'I know. Besides, it's you I've come to see,' Charlotte told her smoothly, sitting down on a hard-backed chair and crossing her legs elegantly to show off their slenderness. 'Just a teensy word of warning... James is mine.' She smiled, showing a row of perfect tiny teeth—like a crocodile's, Lark thought miserably.

'Does he know that?' she responded drily, refusing to allow Charlotte to overpower her.

'Oh, I think so.' She sounded supremely self-confident. 'You see, it's always been understood that we shall marry... Of course, he has his little flings. It's only natural, but normally with women who aren't foolish enough to fall in love with him,' Charlotte added maliciously. 'Poor darling. It came as quite a shock to him last night when I told him...'

There was no way Lark could prevent the wave of faintness from engulfing her; she felt the blood drain away from her skin, leaving her feeling clammy and cold. She was glad that she was sitting down, but even so she had to grip her desk hard to stop herself from swaying.

'What did you say to him?' she demanded fiercely, when she could speak.

Charlotte gave her a supercilious smile. 'Why, only the truth... That you're in love with him. You are, aren't you?'

Lark wasn't going to lie, not this time.

'And if I am?' She tilted her chin firmly. She wasn't going to allow Charlotte to browbeat her.

Charlotte shrugged her shoulders.

'I should have thought a woman with your past would have more intelligence. Oh, I've no doubt that James enjoys taking you to bed. He's a man, after all, and he's always liked variety.' She smiled, the secure, amused smile of a woman who knows her man. 'But that doesn't mean that he sees you as a permanent part of his life. James will marry me.' She lifted her gaze and smiled at Lark with open malice. 'Ask him. I promise you it's the truth. Our engagement is being announced later this year. We'll get married next June.'

'And you'll marry him, knowing that there have been other women?'

Charlotte raised her eyebrows. 'But of course! How middle class you are. James is everything I want in a husband.' She almost purred as she spoke, and a violent feeling of antipathy tore through Lark. She was like a cat enjoying torturing a mouse, she recognised sickly. Charlotte was enjoying doing this to her.

'It's such a very suitable arrangement. James and I will marry. Daddy will settle his estate on both of us. Daddy approves of James. He knows he isn't a fortune-hunter.' She gave Lark a malicious smile and added, 'And of course it's the same for James. He needs a wife who knows how things are done, how to entertain. Aunt Amy is a darling, but so very unworldly. James could go right to the top of the legal profession. Daddy says he's one of the most brilliant prosecuting barristers in the country. But then, of course, I don't have to tell you that, do I? Odd how the case was squashed at the last moment. I asked James if he thought you'd bought off the company...'

'Bought off...' Lark stared at her, unable to believe her ears.

'Not with money, of course.' She smiled acidly. 'There's only one commodity a girl in your position can capitalise on, isn't there? And I do sympathise with you, you know. James is lethal, especially in bed.'

Lark's throat hurt too much for her to make any reply.

Charlotte stood up and smiled dazzlingly. 'I felt it was only fair to tell you, but as I said, if you don't believe me, ask James...'

She left and Lark got up slowly, moving over to the window, hardly able to breathe for the cloying scent of Charlotte's perfume.

It couldn't be true, and yet something deep inside her said that it was. No one, not even Charlotte, would lie about something like that, and challenge her to ask James himself as well. She sat down abruptly. She felt disorientated and confused.

Her first instinct was to confront James with what she knew, but she resisted it. Charlotte's taunt about her falling in love with him had found its mark, and she knew that she couldn't allow herself to be put in the humiliating position of being told that he had lied to her, that his saying he had fallen in love with her had never been anything other than a mere joke.

Much as she longed to just turn and run, she couldn't... Where would she go? How would she live?

The telephone rang. She stared at it as though it was an unfamiliar object, before picking it up and speaking huskily.

'Lark, it's James.'

She gripped the receiver, wondering how it was possible to be so cold and yet perspire so freely at the same time.

'I'm free tonight. I thought we'd go out for dinner, and then back to my place. It's been too long since we've been alone.'

His voice caressed her and she shivered, unable to comprehend his duplicity.

'Lark... Lark, are you still there?'

She could picture him frowning slightly, the dark brows drawn together, the grey eyes silvering with irritation.

It was on the tip of her tongue to tell him that she didn't go out with men who were committed elsewhere, but she didn't trust herself to say the words without bursting into tears. Instead she said huskily, 'I'm afraid I can't, James. A... a prior commitment.'

She hung up before he could argue, and then refused to answer the telephone when it rang again impatiently several minutes later.

In fact, she didn't answer it for the rest of the afternoon, an action which she knew was irresponsible, but she knew she didn't have the courage to speak to him again.

When he burst into her office at five-thirty, she knew she ought to have been prepared, but she wasn't. He looked like a man in the grip of a furious temper, and she shrank back instinctively.

'I never expected you to be a sulker, Lark,' he told her pithily as he crossed the space between them. 'Or to hold a grudge...'

A sulker? A grudge? She opened her mouth, but the hot words of denial and justification never came out; they weren't given the opportunity to do so, because James didn't give it to her.

'All right, so we didn't part on the best of terms yesterday...'

Lark couldn't believe what she was hearing; he actually had the gall to pretend that that was the reason she had refused to see him.

She started to tell him as much, but he wouldn't let her speak, saying harshly instead, 'You aren't going out at all, are you?'

He had trapped her and Lark knew it. She floundered for words, and was rescued by someone tapping on the door.

'There's a gentleman to see you, Miss Cummings,' Cora announced, standing to one side, as Hunter Cabot walked into the room.

He didn't see James at first, exclaiming to Lark, 'At last! I've been trying to reach you all afternoon. I only landed a few hours ago. An unexpected business trip, and I couldn't miss out on the chance...'

'Of taking me to dinner,' Lark supplied rashly, praying that Hunter wouldn't betray her. 'You're earlier than I expected. I haven't even had a chance to get ready yet. Shall I meet you at your hotel? I've forgotten where you said you were staying.'

'The Connaught,' Hunter told her equably. He had realised now that they weren't the only two people in the room, and he turned to James and smiled easily at him. 'Sorry to barge in when you were working, but I've been trying to ring Lark all afternoon to let her know I'd arrived. I just wanted to check that our dinner date was still on. If you'll tell me when you'll be ready, I'll drop by and pick you up.'

'Oh, about half-past eight,' Lark told him, trying to convey her gratitude with her smile, while at the same time unbearably conscious of James's furious stance.

Hunter didn't stay long, probably because he could sense the overheated atmosphere in the study; and of course he must have guessed there was some reason why she had fibbed about them having a date. She wasn't even sure now whether he intended to come back for her or not. She would have to get ready, just in case. At the very least he deserved an explanation for the way she had involved him, Lark decided, as she stood up as calmly as she could and tidied her desk.

'I see,' she heard James say tightly behind her. 'So he doesn't mean a thing to you, does he? My God! And to think I believed you...'

'When I lied?' Lark shot at him. 'Well, I'm not surprised. After all, you didn't when I told the truth.' She felt the bitter sting of tears behind her eyes. 'Perhaps you're not as good as you like to think about differentiating between what's true and what isn't,' she taunted.

A little to her surprise, he went quite pale; a dark, lonely look in his eyes that could only have been a trick of the light, almost making her reach out to him, but she resisted the impulse by thinking of Charlotte.

'No, I don't think I am,' he agreed slowly. He walked toward the door, his movements uncoordinated and jerky.

There was a huge lump in her throat and she longed to call him back, but what good would it do? It was better this way. Better letting him think that she had lied to him all along. At least it would salve her pride.

'You'd better let my mother know if you don't intend coming home tonight,' he told her derisively as he turned at the door, his glance raking her with contempt and dislike, just as he had done once before.

She shivered in the blighting impact of that look for a long time after he had gone. It had underlined to her as nothing else could the vast gulf that lay between reality and what she now saw had been no more than idiotic, romantic daydreams.

Of course he didn't love her—and never would. No man could love a woman at whom he looked the way James had just looked at her.

And it was her own fault. She should have remembered that look, that contempt, and held on to it, instead of allowing herself to be deceived by her own emotions.

All the doubts she had had before returned to grow and crystallise as she went upstairs to get ready to meet Hunter.

Defiantly she put on the silk dress she had worn on the night she and James had made love, refusing to remember how he had looked at her, how he had touched her.

Let him suffer tonight what she had suffered last night, she thought savagely, knowing that his jealousy of Hunter had, like his physical desire for her, been real; but it had only been a male sexual jealousy, that was all. Even so, let him torment himself with mental images of her in Hunter's arms, let him . . . She put down her hairbrush, catching back a sob. What was the use? She didn't want to make him jealous; what she wanted was for the door to open and for him to walk in and tell her that he loved her.

But even if he did say those words, would she believe them after what Charlotte had told her?

Hunter arrived just after eight o'clock. Lark went downstairs to find him talking to Mrs Mayers.

'Ah, Lark! Hunter was just telling me that he's taking you out to dinner.'

Was she imagining it, Lark wondered, or was there really just a hint of coolness in her employer's voice?

She noticed that Mrs Mayers wasn't looking directly at her, and her misery increased. She had gained the impression that Mrs Mayers would have welcomed her as a daughter-in-law, but she must obviously have misunderstood her comments, for she must surely be aware of the truth.

And yet that momentary coolness in her voice seemed to suggest that she did not approve of Lark going out with Hunter.

The moment they were outside, Lark turned to Hunter to explain and apologise, but he refused to let her say a word.

'You don't have to explain a thing,' he assured her. 'I'm just delighted to be having dinner with you.'

He'd booked a table at one of London's more famous restaurants, and Lark recognised several familiar faces from TV and films as they walked in.

Although not normally a drinker, she ordered the champagne cocktail Hunter urged her to try. Perhaps the alcohol might help her to relax.

It must have been stronger than she had anticipated, she decided hazily later on; either that or it hadn't mixed well with the glasses of wine she had consumed.

She looked across the candlelit table at Hunter, reflecting guiltily that she had spent almost the entire evening unburdening herself to him. He had listened in grave silence, intervening only to ask her if she was sure that James and Charlotte were to marry.

'She told me so herself,' she had assured him.

He had frowned a little at that, but had made no comment.

Now she felt absolutely exhausted, even though it was barely eleven o'clock.

'If you don't mind, Hunter, I think I'd like to leave,' she said a little unsteadily.

'Of course. I'll organise a cab.'

He insisted on taking her right to the door, and then asked diffidently if he might take her out again. Much as she liked him, Lark knew that it wasn't fair to either of them for her to agree. Hunter was far too nice a person to be used as a prop for her bruised ego. She shook her head, softening her refusal as best she could by explaining to him how she felt.

What a pity human beings couldn't fall in and out of love to order, she reflected cynically as she went inside and closed the door gently behind her.

CHAPTER TEN

'LARK, there's been a change of plan,' Mrs Mayers came into the study saying a week later. 'We're leaving for Abbotsfield this afternoon. I've organised everything with the caterers and the marquee people. James will be there, too. We'll be staying on for a few days. He wants my advice on some refurbishing he wants carried out, so you'll need to pack a case.'

The crisp tones of her employer's voice surprised Lark as much as her announcement.

When had all this taken place? She had been sitting at her desk all morning and she had had no contact with anyone to suggest that the original date needed to be changed.

Feeling as though she had been derelict in her duties in some way, Lark wanted to ask when these alterations had taken place, but Mrs Mayers had already gone.

She would need the file she had organised for the ball. Where was it? Feeling thoroughly flustered, Lark searched through her desk, finally finding it in its correct place in the filing cabinet. It was already almost lunch time. What time were they actually going to leave? She had attended to the morning post, there was nothing of importance outstanding, so perhaps she ought to go upstairs now and pack.

She refused to allow herself to dwell on what the intimacy of sharing the same house with James was going to do to her.

She would just have to try to keep out of his way.

It shouldn't be too difficult, she thought grimly. He must have spoken with Charlotte by now, and surely must be as anxious to avoid her as she was to avoid him.

175

On the drive down to James's house, Mrs Mayers was quieter than Lark had ever known her to be, giving no explanation as to why the date of their meeting had been changed.

Oxford and its environs wasn't familiar to Lark, and she would have liked to know a little more about the area, if only to keep her mind off James, but Mrs Mayers' silence made her feel reluctant to ask any questions.

They didn't pass through Oxford itself, and Lark soon lost all sense of direction as they traversed country lanes bordered by hedgerows thick with summer green and the froth of creamy-white cow parsley, and then abruptly the house was there, perched on an incline so that it could survey its surroundings. Two Jacobean wings enclosed the original Tudor hall, reaching out like welcoming arms, or at least that was how they appeared to Lark as the car stopped in front of the main entrance.

A plump, smiling woman came out to greet them.

'Lark, this is Mrs Middleton, James's housekeeper,' Mrs Mayers introduced. 'She and her husband look after the house in James's absence.'

Mrs Middleton was in her early forties, with a brisk air that promised efficiency.

'James said he'd be here in time for dinner. I've put you in your usual rooms, Mrs Mayers. James said to put you in the King James room, Miss Cummings,' she told Lark. 'He is reputed to have stayed here once,' she added in explanation, leading the way indoors.

As she followed her, Lark wondered if the whole house had the same air of warmth and welcome that permeated the room she was in.

It must have once been the most important room in the house, she reflected, looking upwards and seeing the minstrels' gallery at one end. Set into the panelling above the huge fireplace was a crest and a Latin motto.

'It's the crest of the family who originally built the house,' Mrs Mayers told her, obviously anticipating her question. 'James's father's family bought it from them during the reign of Queen Victoria... I'm rather tired, Lark. If you don't mind, I think I'll go up to my room and rest.'

She was half-way towards the stairs when Lark asked her urgently, 'The caterers... When are they due to arrive?'

It was Mrs Middleton who answered, assuring her, 'Oh, not for several days yet. You'll have plenty of time to relax and find your feet.'

It seemed an odd comment to make, and equally odd was Mrs Mayers' sudden decision to travel down here, especially when it seemed that their appointments weren't for some time.

Having assured herself that there was nothing Mrs Mayers required, Mrs Middleton turned her attention to Lark, asking her to follow her up the stairs and along a narrow corridor, off which were seven oak doors.

'Here we are,' she announced, turning to open the last one.

She stood back so that Lark could precede her into the room.

It was dominated by a vast four-poster bed, but that was not the reason for Lark's gasp of delight.

Her fingers itched to touch the rich fabric that hung at the windows and covered the bed; polished floor-boards glowed with centuries of beeswax; the afternoon sun shone in through the leaded window. A huge *armoire* stood against one wall, and there was a faint scent of roses in the air. It came, Lark realised, from a bowl of pot pourri standing on the oak chest at the bottom of the bed.

'It's magnificent,' she said softly.

Mrs Middleton smiled.

'I'm glad you like it. James wanted you to have it. It's really the master bedroom, but James has never used it. He says this bed was designed to be shared, not slept in alone.' She laughed and then checked herself uncomfortably. 'I'll go down and make you a pot of tea.'

'I'll come down with you,' Lark told her, adding quietly, 'I am here to work, after all.'

She thought the housekeeper gave her a rather odd look, but she decided she must have imagined it.

James didn't arrive in time for dinner and, despite the fact that she had been dreading seeing him, Lark suffered a sharp stab of disappointment.

Neither she nor Mrs Mayers did justice to the excellent meal Mrs Middleton had provided, and Lark could not blame the housekeeper for frowning slightly when she came in to remove their plates.

'Lark, I'm feeling rather tired. I'm going to have an early night,' murmured Mrs Mayers after the housekeeper had gone.

She would follow suit, Lark decided. That way, she could put off seeing James for almost another day.

She took upstairs with her some papers which showed the number of people who had attended previous fund-raising events organised by the charity.

She had a bath in the luxurious bathroom attached to her bedroom, acknowledging that at another time she would have enjoyed wallowing in the huge Victorian tub which held pride of place in the room, although now it was far less austere than it must have been when it was originally built.

The windowseat was comfortably padded with a fabric to match that in the bedroom; the floor was warmly carpeted; above the custom-made cupboards were mirrors to reflect the light, and the Victorian basin was set into an elegant marble slab.

She dried herself wearily on a thick warm towel, and then pulled on one of her old cotton nightdresses, pulling a wry face at her reflection. She looked all of sixteen years old, with her face free of make-up and her hair curling from the damp heat.

Her white cotton nightdress had a demure bodice threaded with faded blue ribbon. There was a terry-towelling robe hanging up behind the bathroom door and she put it on, letting her bare feet curl into the softness of the carpet as she went back into her bedroom.

The figures she had brought upstairs to study suggested that it should be possible to increase the attendance at the larger events, such as the forthcoming ball, and Lark was just mulling over whether or not it might pay them to advertise the event in some of the glossies, when someone rapped briefly on her bedroom door.

It opened before she was out of her chair, and the sight of James striding determinedly towards her made her grab at the chair itself to stop herself from stumbling.

'James! What...what are you doing in here?'

She knew it was an idiotic question the moment she uttered it, and was not surprised to hear him reply sardonically, 'It does happen to be my home, and since you've spent the last few days determinedly refusing to see or speak to me, I decided the only way I was going to get to find out exactly what's going on was to get you down here.'

Get her down here! All her suspicions about the suddenness with which the existing arrangements had been changed coalesced, and she demanded disbelievingly, 'Are you trying to tell me that you went to all the trouble of changing those appointments, of upsetting your mother's arrangements, just to speak to me?'

His mouth twisted slightly. 'You didn't leave me much alternative.'

Lark started to tremble. This was the last thing she had expected. After Charlotte's disclosures, she had expected James to accept that, since she knew the truth, there could be no continuation of their relationship.

In Boston he had told her he was in love with her. And she had believed him—almost. But how could he be in love with her, and yet intending to marry Charlotte?

'Besides,' she heard him add, as though he had picked up on her train of thought, 'you still owe me two weeks.'

'Two weeks?'

'You promised me two months,' he reminded her softly, his expression suddenly savagely bitter as he caught hold of her, gripping her arms through the thick terry-towelling so hard that she flinched. 'You also told me that Cabot meant nothing to you.'

'So we both lied.' Lark lifted her chin.

His anger was dangerously exciting, because beneath it she could sense his pent-up desire. He still wanted her. Another woman in her shoes might have felt triumph, she reflected, but all she could feel was a sick bewilderment that he was not the man she had thought, after all.

She ought to have stuck to her original assessment of him, instead of letting her judgement become clouded with emotion.

'I think you'd better leave, James,' she told him, struggling to overcome both the imprisoning grip of his fingers and the treacherous awareness of him that was stealing over her own senses.

Another few seconds of being close to him like this, able to breathe in the unique male scent of his skin, to see the dark arousal of his eyes, and she would be clinging unashamedly to him, begging him to make love to her.

'Surely you aren't afraid of being alone with me,' he taunted, deliberately misunderstanding.

Lark stood her ground. 'Why should I be?' she countered.

She ought to have remembered how skilled he was with words, because the next thing she knew her prison had tightened around her, and she could feel the quick, heavy beat of his heart against her body as he said softly, 'Because of this...'

She knew that he was going to kiss her; she could have avoided the drugging pressure of his mouth seducing her own, but she had thought if she could just stand cold

and unresponding beneath it, that would show him more
than any amount of words how she felt, but instead . . .

Instead she felt the unmistakable arousal of her body,
its instinctive yearning towards him, the aching pull of
her senses that demanded that she give in to the in-
sidious lure of his touch.

For a while she did, drowning in the pleasure of being
close to him, of touching him, of knowing that he was
held in thrall to his desire for her almost as she was to
her love for him, but then she pulled away, catching him
off guard so that he released her.

'No, James,' she told him huskily, avoiding looking
directly at him. 'It's over. I told you in Boston I can't
have a relationship with a man I can't trust.'

'You're going to hold that damn court case over my
head like a sword for ever, aren't you?' he snarled back,
anger mingling with his frustration. 'I never thought
you'd be so small-minded, Lark. For God's sake, I was
doing my job, and when I . . .'

'I don't want to talk about it any more,' Lark told
him, cutting across what he was going to say.

Oh, God, even now he couldn't be honest with her,
couldn't admit the truth. She ached to tackle him with
it, to throw his involvement with Charlotte at him like
a time bomb, but the last thing she wanted to do was to
involve herself in the role of a jealous woman, even
though that was exactly what she was.

'I don't want *you* any more,' she threw at him bitterly.

It was the wrong thing to say.

One moment she was standing free and safe, the next
she was imprisoned between the wall and his body, all
too aware of his angry arousal as she tried to squirm
away and to stop him from stripping off her robe.

'So you don't want me, do you?' he said thickly. 'We'll
just see about that . . .'

Mingling with her outrage and fear was just the
tiniest, scorching humiliating thread of triumph.

He leaned into her, making her acutely aware of his hard body, neither of them even hearing the soft rap on the door, or aware that they weren't alone any more until Lark heard Mrs Mayers exclaiming in a shocked voice, 'James!'

Her face scarlet with mortification and guilt, Lark snatched up her robe and pulled it on. Her nightdress was perfectly respectable, but the scene had spoken for itself.

That James did not share her inhibitions was perfectly obvious from the way he said sardonically to his mother, 'Just in the nick of time, Mother. Although somehow I doubt that ultimately it would have been rape.'

The ugly, unkind words hurt Lark more than anything else he had done. She turned her head away quickly, hoping to conceal her feelings.

James, she noticed, was keeping his back to his mother as he walked towards the door, and she shivered a little, remembering the aroused heat of his body against her own. Even now part of her mourned its loss.

'I wanted to have a word with you, Lark, but it will wait until morning,' she heard Mrs Mayers say just before the door closed behind both mother and son.

Once they had gone, Lark flung herself face down on her bed, wishing she could find relief for her feelings in tears.

She was still lying there half an hour later when she felt a light touch on her shoulder.

'Lark, I've made us a pot of tea. You and I need to talk.'

Mrs Mayers!

Lark sat up clumsily.

'Lark, what's gone wrong between you and James? You seemed so happy...'

'I found out that he's going to marry Charlotte,' Lark told her bluntly, beyond pretending that she had been naïve enough to imagine that James saw his future with her.

'What?' There was no mistaking the shock in Mrs Mayers' voice. 'Where on earth did you get that idea? Not from James. I happen to know that the only woman he wants for his wife is you,' Mrs Mayers told her robustly.

'But Charlotte told me herself...'

'She's lying,' Mrs Mayers said crisply. 'Oh, I don't doubt she believes she wants to marry him, but James has never thought of her as anything more than an adopted sister or cousin. When did she tell you this?'

'Some time ago.'

'And you said nothing to James?' Mrs Mayers sounded both shocked and a little angry. 'Lark, my dear, I promised James I wouldn't interfere, but he *is* my son and I can't bear to see him so unhappy. Please be honest with me now. Is it just because Charlotte lied to you that you've been refusing to see him, or was that just a convenient excuse?'

Lark shook her head.

'I love James, but...' She looked at Mrs Mayers despairingly. 'I feel I don't really know him...not as a person...and he doesn't know me.'

'He loves you,' Mrs Mayers told her quietly. 'He wants to make you his wife. He told me that before...' She broke off and looked confused, flushing a little.

'How *can* he love me?' Lark protested. 'He still believes I was involved in Gary's fraud. I know he does... He never talks about it, but it's still there. When he was in court...' She shuddered violently and bent her head.

'Lark, my dear, I'm going to break a confidence and tell you something I promised I wouldn't.' There was a moment's pause, and then Mrs Mayers said very clearly, 'Lark, it was *because* of James that the court decided not to pursue the case. He told his clients that anyone could see that you were completely innocent, that you had been brutally victimised and used as a scapegoat, and he refused to continue with the case. *That* was why it was dismissed!'

The room swung wildly round her; Lark stared at Mrs Mayers disbelievingly.

'That isn't true,' she whispered, suddenly looking haunted. 'It can't be! James would have said...'

Mrs Mayers shook her head. 'No, my dear...he would not have said. You see, he fell in love with you on sight. Believe me, he found it quite a shock. He came to see me after the first day you were called up in court. He told me that the moment he saw you he'd been struck by two things; the first, that you were the most beautiful girl he'd ever seen, and the second, that you were so obviously innocent that he couldn't understand how the case had ever gone so far. He also told me that it would be next to impossible for him to win your trust because in court you had been terrified of him, or rather, of his reputation. He asked me for my help. He knew you had no job, nowhere to live.' She frowned slightly. 'He knew I needed an assistant and begged me to give you the job.

'I did point out to him that to deceive you by asking me not to let you guess that I was his mother was hardly conducive to gaining your trust, but he told me that he intended to tell you the truth.'

Lark remembered how he had come to see her at her bedsit. Perhaps if she hadn't panicked then he would have told her. As it was, she had hardly given him the opportunity to do so, she reflected unhappily.

'But why didn't he *tell* me that he was responsible for the case being dismissed?' she protested huskily.

'Perhaps because he didn't want to put any undue pressure on you,' Mrs Mayers suggested kindly. 'Lark, is it so impossible to believe that he wanted you to love him for himself—not out of gratitude, or any misplaced sense of responsibility?'

She ought to have guessed, to have known. There had been so many small pointers, so much evidence to show her how different he was from the hard, uncaring man she had first imagined. So much heartache, and all for nothing. But it wasn't too late...

Lark got up unsteadily.

'I must go and see him. Where is he?'

'In the library. I'm afraid he isn't in a very good mood,' Mrs Mayers warned her. 'He thinks that you've rejected him in favour of Hunter.'

'I know. It was the only way I could think of saving face.'

Mrs Mayers got up too, and kissed her warmly.

'I shall tell him that I know...about everything,' Lark told her firmly, and then added softly, 'But after I've told him how much I love him.'

The library was in the Jacobean part of the house; a huge rectangular room with bookcases on three walls, and panelling and a large open fire on the fourth.

James was sitting in front of it with his back to her, his head bent forward, his hands locked. He hadn't heard her come in.

She got two-thirds of the way across the room before he saw her. The look he gave her was so bleak and withdrawn that she almost lost her courage, but she owed him this if nothing else, and so, gripping her hands together, she said quickly, 'James, I love you very, very much, and I want to spend the rest of my life with you. I want to have your children, and share your life, and if your mother's wrong and you don't really love me at all, please tell me now, before I make an even greater fool of myself than I already have.'

For a moment she thought he intended to ignore her, and then he asked curtly, 'What brought on this change of heart? Less than an hour ago I was the last person you wanted in your life.'

'I discovered that you aren't going to marry Charlotte,' she told him simply.

He got up then, shock dispersing his original anger, and she could see that she had surprised him. 'How in hell did you get hold of a crazy idea like that?' He saw her face and smiled grimly. 'Ah, I see. My God, I shall have something to say to that young woman the next time I see her. Charlotte never has and never will mean anything more to me than, at best, a rather irritating younger sister. Although, to be truthful, if she *was* my sister, I suspect that she'd have felt the flat of my hand against her rear end long before now! Her father, on the other hand, is a man I admire and respect a great deal. Charlotte is his only child. I am one of her trustees in the event of his death. He worries because even he can see that she hasn't got the least scrap of sense.'

'She loves you,' Lark told him huskily.

He shook his head.

'No, she wants me. Like a child wanting a new toy because it's out of reach.'

'You took her out to dinner.'

'She certainly made capital out of that, didn't she? It was a twenty-first birthday party for a friend of hers, and I'd agreed a long time ago that I would escort her. A promise which I cursed most thoroughly when I realised it was going to deprive me of an evening of your company, but you see, my darling, when I agreed to go with her I hadn't even met you.'

'Nor fallen in love with me across a crowded court room?' Lark suggested tentatively.

He seemed to read her mind because, instead of denying it, he smiled ruefully.

'Ah, I see Mother has been talking. I'm not surprised you find it hard to believe, though. I had a little trouble coming to terms with it myself. Lawyers pride themselves on their ability to reason, and believe me there wasn't and there isn't anything the slightest bit reasonable about the way I feel about you. I ought to beat you for what you've put us both through,' he added roughly.

Lark gave him a mischievous smile, reassured by the passionate look he was giving her. 'Can't I persuade you to get the case dismissed?'

She saw from his face that he knew what she was trying to tell him.

'Mother *has* been talking, hasn't she?' He was frowning now, turning slightly away from her. 'Let's get one thing straight, Lark. I refused to continue with the case, not because I'd fallen in love with you, but because I knew you were innocent. Had I not thought so, even though I would still have loved you, I *would* have continued with the prosecution.'

He looked at her then, a hard, direct look that challenged her to either accept or reject him on his principles.

'I wouldn't expect you to do anything else,' Lark told him huskily. 'You frightened me in court, James.' She ignored his wry 'I know' to continue, 'But what has worried me through our relationship was the fact that you wouldn't talk about it. It made me doubt that you could really love me, because I believed that you thought I was guilty.'

'And I thought *you* didn't trust me because of what happened in court, and yet I didn't want to tell you why the case had been dismissed because, knowing your history, I could see how easy it would be then for you to feel guilty, and for you to feel that you had to love me, if only in repayment, and that wasn't what I wanted. As it was, I had a large enough burden on my conscience for rushing you into a physical relationship before you'd had time to get to know me,' he added roughly.

'We're both at fault,' Lark consoled him. 'We should both have been more honest...had more faith.'

'Well, in that case, I have to admit that I got Mother to bring you down here under false pretences. I was desperate to get you away from Cabot, and to have one last attempt to convince you that we could have a good future together.'

'Hunter was never any threat to you,' Lark told him lovingly, going on to explain about Hunter's fortuitous arrival in London.

'Well, there aren't going to be any more misunderstandings of that nature,' James told her firmly. 'And just to make sure, I think you and I should get married. After all, you're already occupying the Bride's Chamber.'

Lark looked puzzled. 'I thought it was called the King James room.'

'So it is, because during his visit he occupied the best bedroom in the house, but that bed was bought for his bride by the same Jacobean Lacey who built on the two extra wings, and every bride has slept there since.'

He kissed her gently, and then far less gently, releasing her with reluctance.

'I think we'd better go and tell my mother that she can stop playing *deus ex machina*, before she comes looking for us.'

He kissed her again and then put his arm around her, to hold her against his side, as they walked towards the door.

Two months later Mrs Middleton was standing beside the verger's wife as they both watched the newly married couple emerging from the church.

It was a perfect September day, warm and sunny, with the trees just beginning to turn. The bride looked radiant in the heavy satin dress that had been made especially for her in London. Her veil had been loaned by her new mother-in-law, and its creamy lace suited her vivid colouring to perfection.

'I knew the moment he asked me to prepare the Bride's Chamber for her what was going on,' Mrs Middleton exclaimed happily. 'Mind you, I was a bit surprised that she wasn't wearing a ring that first time I saw her, and when she told me she had come to work... But then I suppose they wanted to keep it to themselves for a while...'

'They're off to America for their honeymoon,' the verger's wife responded.

'Yes, Mrs Mayers has a house near Boston.' She sighed again. 'You should have seen the way they looked at one another when she offered to lend it to them! My, it quite took me back to my own courting days.'

Both women gave exclusively feminine and satisfied sighs.

Lark floated down the ancient church path on James's arm while the bells rang triumphantly around them. He kissed her by the lych gate, much to the delight of their guests, and murmured under his breath, 'Got you sentenced at last, Mrs Wolfe.'

Lark laughed and responded, 'For a lifetime.'

Harlequin Presents.

Coming Next Month

#1207 JOURNEY BACK TO LOVE Rachel Elliot
Leigh is astounded when actor Slade Keller, known for his aversion to the press, agrees to an interview—but only with Leigh. A refusal means her job. Yet there is no way she can explain her past involvement with Slade—or her deception of him.

#1208 MADELEINE'S MARRIAGE Emma Goldrick
When Joel Fairmont moves into the house next door, successful estate agent Madeleine Charbonneau's life changes abruptly. Unromantic, hardworking, it just isn't like her to threaten a stranger with violence—but then, other strangers hadn't kissed her like that!

#1209 STRANDED HEART Vanessa Grant
Having had one marriage break up very publicly, Nicole fears getting involved again. So the last thing she needs is Matt Kealey, a wild mountain man with no plans to stay in one place for long—especially when he remembers the scandal of her past.

#1210 DARK MOSAIC Anne Mather
She was called Jessica Devlin, and she had been traveling north to claim her inheritance. Or so they told her after the train crash. But she can't remember anything. Everyone is kind, especially her late father's cousin, James Bentley—yet why does she feel so ill at ease?

#1211 ANOTHER TIME Susan Napier
Helen knows she's never met Alex Knight before, even though he's the brother of the man she's about to marry. Yet Alex claims they had been lovers five years ago in Hong Kong—and that if Helen marries Greg, she'll be making an enormous mistake.

#1212 SPARRING PARTNERS Elizabeth Oldfield
Shelly travels to the tropical island of Nevis to change David Llewellyn's low opinion of her. Somehow, her efforts seem doomed to failure. How can she convince him she's not—and never was—a con woman?

#1213 A LAW UNTO HIMSELF Frances Roding
Being jilted by Paolo di Calaveri is the best thing that could have happened to Francesca. It frees her from her domineering grandfather and forces her to make choices about her life. And one of those involves the cynical, equally domineering Oliver Newton.

#1214 YESTERDAY'S EMBERS Sandra K. Rhoades
Lesley hadn't heard about Zack since their divorce five years ago. But she can't send him away when he arrives with a horse for their daughter's birthday. He still has an incredible effect on Lesley's emotions—could things be different between them now?

Available in October wherever paperback books are sold, or through Harlequin Reader Service:

In the U.S.
901 Fuhrmann Blvd.
P.O. Box 1397
Buffalo, N.Y. 14240-1397

In Canada
P.O. Box 603
Fort Erie, Ontario
L2A 5X3

Have You Ever Wondered If You Could Write A Harlequin Novel?

Here's great news—Harlequin is offering a series of cassette tapes to help you do just that. Written by Harlequin editors, these tapes give practical advice on how to make your characters—and your story—come alive. There's a tape for each contemporary romance series Harlequin publishes.

Mail order only

All sales final

TO:
Harlequin Reader Service
Audiocassette Tape Offer
P.O. Box 1396
Buffalo, NY 14269-1396

I enclose a check/money order payable to HARLEQUIN READER SERVICE® for $9.70 ($8.95 plus 75¢ postage and handling) for EACH tape ordered for the total sum of $ _____
Please send:

- [ ] Romance and Presents
- [ ] American Romance
- [ ] Temptation
- [ ] Intrigue
- [ ] Superromance
- [ ] All five tapes ($38.80 total)

Signature _____

Name: _____
(please print clearly)

Address: _____

State: _____ Zip: _____

* Iowa and New York residents add appropriate sales tax.

AUDIO-H